ACKNOWLEDGEMENTS

The author gratefully acknowledges the help and advice of:—

Emrys Bryson	— Nottingham Evening Post.
Walter Hayes	— Charter Bookseller, Beeston.
Tony McCourt	— Spectrum Graphics
Mrs Truus Taminiau	— Hudson's Bookshop, Milton Street, Nottm.
Lance Tarlton-Weatherall	— John Menzies Library Services Ltd.

G000232540

First Edition

© Joan Wallace 1984

ISBN 0 947790 00 4

Typeset by Spectrum Graphics (Nottm.) Ltd, Nottingham.
Printed by Printhouse Ltd., Langley Mill, Nottingham.
Cover design by Hilary Evans

Published by Gowan Publishing Ltd, Nottingham.

FOREWORD

The canvas of life on which Joan Wallace paints is hard, tough, and coarse. That's the way life was in Radford in the thirties.

But on this uncompromising material she has managed to produce a picture of touching tenderness. Vera and her husband Jack are, by the world's lights, nobody special. Their everyday worries, the constant struggle to make ends meet, the fear that the wife will get "caught" by another baby, are commonplace in their class and in their time.

Even their tragedies are not unique. But there is a resilience about this Nottingham working-class couple which seems typical of their kind.

And with an ear and eye for authenticity, Joan Wallace puts down — with simplicity and honesty — what they are like and what their life is like. By the end of the book, we feel that we have always known them. What more could one ask?

NOTTINGHAM EVENING POST

About the Author

Joan Wallace has lived in Nottingham all her life and was educated at the Bentinck Road Secondary and William Crane schools.

She has written over one hundred short stories — many of these have been published in the London Evening News, Nottingham Evening Post, Woman's Own and various other magazines. Her regional stories have been broadcast on radios Nottingham, Derby and Trent. She has won the Silver Jubilee Cup presented by The Nottingham Writers' Club for the best radio story and has been awarded their Writer of the Year award.

The author is also an entertainer and has written a book about her experiences in the pubs and clubs in and around Nottingham — the book is to be published in 1985.

For

Walter Scanlon

Best wishes from
Joan Wallace

INDEPENDENT STREET

by

Joan Wallace

CHAPTER ONE

"Push harder...come on harder, it's nearly there. Go on, it's all right duck, you can scream your head off if you want to, don't mind me. That's it, let them hear that top 'C'. It's going to be a right whopper by the looks of things."

The midwife held on to the writhing woman's ankles and made sure the legs stayed wide apart.

"Ooh, you have got some lungs on you, duck. You're giving your old man a right fright down there, might put him off for a few weeks! I can see the head! Come on now...just a few more pushes! There's a nice cup of tea for you when you've finished."

Vera Denbey closed her eyes and making sure her tongue and the insides of her cheeks were out of the way, she clenched her teeth together, held her breath and pushed down...down...down and thought that with all the strength she was putting behind the push she could have moved a tram-car single-handed.

"Gotyer, my little beauty!" The midwife tugged at the baby's head. "I've got him...come on now, duck...give me some help with the last bit." She pulled again and Vera felt as if her body was being ripped apart. Never again, she thought through the thick haze of pain, this will be the last, the very last. Never, never again will I go through this hell. The midwife pulled the baby into the world and said, "It's another lad. Another lad for you and just look at the size of him. I'll bet he's a ten pounder." She held the baby upside down with its feet and looked like a triumphant fisherman holding a record catch up for a photograph to be taken.

The baby did not respond to this indignity but kept his mouth tightly clasped together; a dead thing.

The midwife gave him a slap on the bottom and as though he had been awakened from a lovely, cosy sleep, the baby opened his mouth and protested loudly with a quivering yell.

"Oh dear, oh dear, what a noise." The midwife's fingers flittered over him: cleaning; searching for abnormalities; caressing. She smiled down at the exhausted Vera. "Sometimes it seems like I'm never going to escape from noise. My job's all noise, do you know that! If it isn't the mothers screaming their heads off, it's their babies. Noise, noise, noise. And I don't even get away from it when I go to bed. My old man snores half the night — he sounds just like two pigs having a fight when he gets going."

She gently wiped the baby's eyes with cottonwool, then wrapped him in the piece of clean sheet which had been cut up ready. She placed him at Vera's breast and said, "Here you are, shove a titty in his mouth and shut him up. I'll just clean you up a bit then we'll have that nice cup of tea."

After a while the midwife walked to the bedroom door and shouted down the stairs, "Are you there, Mr. Denbey! We're ready for that tea now, and keep that hot water going...you can bring some more up now. Oh, you've got another son by the way."

Jack Denbey poured the boiling water into the wash basin and looked across to the bed. Hair tousled, eyes listless and puffy through lack of sleep, he smiled at Vera and said softly, "You worked that nicely, love. I shan't have to have any time off now. Are you all right? You're all right are you..... and the little lad?"

Vera treated him to a smile and nodded but she did not let him into the secret monologue that was going on inside her head. She felt too weak to talk but her mind kept on going.

Jack seemed grateful to escape from the room as he hurried off to make the tea. Vera closed her eyes again and thought, All right, am I all right! Huh, he's the one who ought to go through this lot. Married three years and a baby every year. I'm twenty-five and should be enjoying myself. I know I got married later than all my friends but still, I couldn't leave mam on her own. I had to wait 'til she got married again. Mind you, I have been repaid a hundredfold. Mam's always a big help when I have a baby, couldn't do without her. And look how she always sees after the others when I'm giving birth! She'll be round soon, basket filled with home-made bread and chicken-broth and anything else she's been able to beg and cadge. Oh, I don't suppose I ought to worry like I do. Things always work out. Jack's got his job at the cigarette factory. Money's nothing to shout about, but at least we can pay our dues and demands...that's more than a lot of them can do round here. But three babies in three years! Perhaps this one will die! If this one died I could have a breathing space from nappies and feeds and endless crying! I never wanted him......never wanted the others come to that. It's all Jack's fault — he's always at me. Anybody'd think I was a machine. But that's marriage I suppose — that's what you get married for. Oh my God!" She shuddered and the horror of her thoughts made her clench her teeth together again. "In about six weeks time he will be at me again. Properly that is, doing everything. It was Thursday today, but by Saturday he would start touching her again and stroking her poor swollen breasts. All that horrible touching that nearly drove her mad. He could not seem to help himself. Pregnancy and childbirth seemed to make him desire her more than ever. She imagined Jack climbing on top of her, his mouth wide open moist with excitement jibbering rubbish as his passion took control of him. She moaned out aloud and the midwife hurried over to her.

"What's the matter, duck, where's it hurting you?" Vera wanted to laugh. What a question! The woman must be a bit soft in the head. She wanted to yell at her, "Everywhere's hurting....every single place in my body that has any feeling in it is hurting." But instead she said weakly, "Baby sucked a bit hard that's all....my nipple's tender."

Jack returned to the bedroom carrying three cups of tea on a tray. He placed one on the bedside cabinet for Vera.

The midwife went downstairs to get a packet of cigarettes from her handbag.

Jack sat down on the edge of the bed and leaned over the baby who was still sucking life into himself as though sensing he was resented by his life-giver.

"You're both beautiful," Jack kissed Vera on the forehead and rubbed his thumb across her breasts then gently stroked the baby's face. "Glorious womanhood, that's what you are, love. Woman in all her glory they say don't they! This is what women glory in."

Vera decided right at that very moment that Jack's glorious manhood was going to take a few knocks. No more babies in this house and that was absolutely certain. She had to have a plan, some sort of scheme. Like old generals have when they're plotting strategy.

"Lovely cup of tea, Jack." She held the cup away from the baby. "Isn't it time you were setting off for work? Mam'll be here soon so you needn't worry about me."

She looked down at her child — he was falling gently to sleep and frowning at the whole business. Vera felt the familiar protectiveness creeping through her body and all at once wanted to cry when she remembered how she had wished the tiny child dead. She kissed the down of hair on his head and nuzzled him like a mare with her foal. He was beautiful....perfection.

Jack left for work after the midwife had been paid her money and the midwife hurried off to her next 'noisy mother'.

Vera looked down at her sleeping child again and whispered to him, "I'm sorry....it's got nothing to do with you, darling....I didn't mean it, not for one minute. And to prove it to you I'm going to give you extra special love. You'll be the lucky one, you'll see." She stroked his forehead with the tips of her fingers, traced the network of frowns. Now, how does that rhyme go! I think it goes —

> *Monday's child is fair of face*
> *Tuesday's child is full of grace*
> *Wednesday's child is full of woe*
> *Thursday's child has far to go*

That's you....Thursday's child....you're going to go far my darling. And I shall give you a good name....a lucky name. You'll be named after someone great. She thought her way through a list of names. "I know what we'll call you! Alexander! After Alexander-the-Great! I'll bet you'll be the only boy in Radford with the name Alexander. Ey up....that sounds like your grandma's here." Her mother did not approve of the name. She wanted him to be another Joseph like her first husband, or an Alfred like her second.

"I'll tell you what we'll do," Vera compromised, "we'll name him Alexander Joseph. Now, pull that chair up close, I want some advice. What was it you said Mrs. Davenport used....to stop her falling for a baby?"

Mother and daughter plotted quietly together and if Jack could have heard them his faith in glorious womanhood would have been catapulted slightly off course.

"She swears by it," Maisie chuckled, "and she reckons her husband don't mind. But I bet they have to make sure neither of them have got any cuts anywhere. It'd sting a fair bit wouldn't it!"

They both roared with laughter and Alexander Joseph whimpered in his sleep as though taking part in the fun.

"Cottonwool and vinegar," Vera laughed weakly, "it'll be cheap enough anyway. And I can always water the vinegar down a bit like they do at the chip-shop."

"Ooh, you are a one, our Vera. Hey, I'd better make a start on the dinner. Alf and the lads'll be wanting their dinners soon and I've done nothing here yet. Alf's got a job caddying for some toff on Wollaton Park this afternoon so I can fetch his best suit out of pawn tomorrow. My lady's having a dinner party on Saturday night as well, so I should be able to get hold of some chicken bits for your dinner. She might give me some sherry again, like she did the last time I told her you'd had a baby. If she does, I'll pop round when I've finished on Saturday night and we'll have a little party of our own. Oh dear, I've done nothing yet, nothing." Maisie bustled off down the stairs.

"Oh yes you have, mam," thought Vera, "you've cheered me up and given me help." She talked to her sleeping child. "You know what you are don't you. With a bit of luck you're the 'Last of the Mohicans'."

She closed her eyes once again and joined her baby in the land of sleep.

Vera slept peacefully for a while and so did Alexander and at 12-0 o'clock Maisie prepared a light meal for Vera. She warmed up the chicken soup and cut three thin slices of brown bread. She took a tray from out of the dresser in the kitchen and smiled as she ran her finger-tips along the top of the dresser. Even at a time like this the house was spotless. Vera was as particular in pregnancy as a bird was with its nest or a cat with its newspapers. Everywhere spotlessly clean and highly polished.

"Takes after her mam for that," Maisie muttered proudly to herself as she mashed a fresh pot of tea.

She placed the soup and tea things on the tray and walked carefully up the stairs.

"Here you are, love. Some nice chicken soup with plenty of big chunks in it and some brown bread cut lovely and wafer thin, just how you used to like it when you were poorly in bed with the measles and chickenpox when you were little."

Maisie placed the tray on the bed and held out her arms for the baby. "Let's have him then." She lifted him gently into her arms and kissed his forehead. "Oh, I could eat him. Isn't he a lovely little thing. Do you know Vera, he's the spittin' image of your dad! There look....across the eyes and the nose." Her eyes filled with tears. "It's just like your dad's been born all over again."

Vera propped herself up with the pillows and sipped at the chicken soup. "I've got to have stitches, mam. The midwife's sending the doctor this afternoon." She sighed and looked at the ceiling. "More money to pay out."

"I'm not surprised you've got to have stitches....look at the size of him the great dumpling. He's like a baby of three months or more, my arms are beginning to ache already, they are. It's right what they say you know."

"What who say?" Vera dipped a slice of bread in the soup.

"They make your arms ache when they're little and your heart ache when they're big."

"I haven't made your heart ache have I, mam!" Vera looked amused.

"No, you haven't, but your three brothers made up for it." Maisie kissed Alexander on the forehead again. "I don't know....you go through hell giving birth to them....go without to clothe them and bring them up nice....and all for what! So that they can be maimed and blinded and killed by strangers in a foreign country. If I had my time over again and know what I know now I should never have had any children at all. It's too much for people to go through it is. It's a wonder I didn't end up in Mapperley having to go through that lot. Husband and three lovely sons all killed....and for what....for what Vera!" Her face went white and the lines on her forehead grew deeper as the horror of it clutched at her mind.

"Did you say your lady's giving another dinner party on Saturday?" Vera had grown adept at steering Maisie away from the excrutiatingly painful memories of the past and she needed to do so for her own sake too because she had been very fond of her three elder brothers and devoted to her father. "See if you can get a bit of that ham like last time. It melted in your mouth and the fat was lovely and sweet. I could really fancy a bit of ham like that. If we were rich I would have ham for tea every day of the week."

"I'll see what there is going." The ploy had worked, Maisie forgot the men for a while and started to chatter about the dinner party which was being held by her employers — a bank manager and his wife. "I'm helping Mrs. Guest with some of the cooking so I'll see what I can cadge for you. As I said, I know they're having chicken so I'll get some bits, and the carcass for some more soup. And they're having chocolate pudding because it's Mrs. Brown's favourite and I'll be sure to make a big one so's there'll be some left over. You can soon get Jack to warm it up and make a bit of custard."

"Oh, I love their chocolate pudding. I could just eat a bit now." Vera's eyes looked extra bright at the thought of chocolate pudding.

"And I'll try and sneak a bit of pork-pie out for the men's suppers. Alf goes mad over a bit of pork-pie. He likes the jelly bit best."

"I don't know what we'd all do without you, mam." Vera wiped the soup bowl clean with the last piece of crust. "That was lovely, fit for a queen. Is there any left for Jack? You know what men are like....he can't look after himself very well."

Maisie placed Alexander in his cot at the side of the bed then poured two cups of tea.

"Here's your tea and don't start whittling about Jack. He won't starve you know, I've never known it yet. And he gets a good dinner in the work's canteen don't he! They reckon that their canteen is the finest in the country. They look after the workers better than anywhere. I wish Alf could get set on there, but you ought to see the queues outside every morning. Your Jack's very lucky to have a job there, he wants to hang on to it. And look at the good bonus they get every March! You'll be able to go to Skeggy again next year for the day when he gets his bonus."

"Yes, you're right I suppose, but you know he's not ever so happy. What I mean to say is....he's always on about going in the offices. He'd much rather work in the offices instead of being a machine driver. He says you can get on better if you can get a job in the offices. Or start your own business."

"Ah well....he wants to hang on to what he's got, no mind having fancy ideas. There's queues full of men on the dole who'd snatch his hand off for his job." Maisie glanced at the bedside clock.

"Now you drink your tea and settle down again. And I'll do Jack's tea when I bring the boys back later on. Doctor'll be here before long to do his fancy needlework on you." She chuckled and patted at her hair.

"I know and I'm dreading it. I keep blushing everytime I think about it. I wish he was a lady doctor then it wouldn't seem so bad."

"Ooh," Maisie laughed, "if old doctor Johnson was a lady doctor he'd have something to worry about an' all. Now don't be so daft," Maisie put her hand on Vera's hand and squeezed it, trying to convey comfort and support through the contact of flesh....mother and daughter. "He won't even notice, he'll be in such a hurry. Doctors are always rushed off their feet you know, in September they are. Everybody's needing doctors and stitches this time of year."

Vera looked puzzled and asked, "What do you mean this time of year? How do you know who's having a baby and who isn't?"

"Christmas!" Maisie put the pots onto the tray. "It's simple isn't it! That's when everybody goes mad, at Christmas. All the husbands want a bit of love at Christmas and with all that drinking and merrymaking....well they're not too careful about what they're doing are they! That's when you and Jack slipped up isn't it, around Christmastime!"

Vera blushed and nodded her head. "There you are then, I told you." Maisie bent over the sleeping Alexander. "And here's your little Christmas present....all tucked up in his little manger," she bent closer, "aren't you, me duck. And if you don't watch it, Vera — Jack'll be giving you another Christmas-box this year as well. You make sure you use some commonsense in future....and some cottonwool-and-vinegar."

They both laughed and Vera rolled her eyes and screwed up her face in mock agony.

"Oh....don't get on about that, mam....not when I've got to have stitches. You'll put me off for life."

"It's Jack who wants putting off for life, but you haven't got much hope of that, love. Even when you get to my age you have your work cut out putting them off." She picked up the tea tray and walked to the top of the stairs. "I'll see you later then, Vera. Doctor'll let himself in won't he! He'll soon have you in stitches."

Vera laughed weakly and sank down into the sanctuary of the bedclothes. Alexander Joseph slept on, oblivious to all the bother he had caused.

"Arms ache when they're little....and heartache when they're big." Vera whispered to him, "I've got a very strong heart, my darling."

★★★★★★★★★★★★

CHAPTER TWO

Maisie decided to walk back to her house and save the tramcar fare. She nipped down Edinburgh Street, then on to Connaught Street and past the Notman Pram Company with its sweet smell of freshly sawn wood which was intermingled with the sickly aroma emanating from the Barnett sweet factory. Just before she reached Denman Street she stopped to talk to an old Jewish lady who was sitting on a chair in the doorway of her house.

"Hello, Mrs. Cohen....it's another little lad. That's three she's got now you know."

"Aah," Mrs. Cohen nodded her head and swayed gently from side-to-side, "a boy God bless him. You bring him to see me, don't forget!"

Maisie smiled at Mrs. Cohen then continued to the corner and on to Denman Street, then after a while she reached St. Peters Street and was back in Sodom within a few minutes of leaving Vera's house.

Past the River Leen that waved hello with its dark green weeds, over the Penny Weigh-Bridge, up the hill past Radford Railway Station, then she turned right at Canterbury Road.

"Gramarr....Gramarr!" Frankie toddled to greet her as she entered Chesil Avenue. He was dressed in a sailor suit and swayed from side-to-side in his hurry to reach Maisie, looking like a drunken sailor who had shrunk to doll size.

Dougie was safely ensconced in his pram parked outside the front door but he held out his arms to Maisie and strained at the reigns like a horse rearing-to-go in a race.

"Hello me ducks, hello," Maisie scooped Frankie up into her arms and gave Dougie a squeeze. "Guess what! I've just been to your house and you know that stork I was telling you about! Well....he's been to your house this morning and brought you a little baby brother."

"Little stork," said Frankie excitedly, "I want to look at the stork." Dougie backed him up with a few grunts and some ventriloquist-like conversation.

"You've got a new baby brother," Maisie persisted, "and you'll see him at teatime."

"Where's the stork?" insisted Frankie.

"Oh, he's flown away again," Maisie laughed into his neck. "He's got to deliver a lot more babies today."

Alf's voice boomed out at her, "Better not let me catch it round here. I'll shoot the bogger."

"Oh, hark who's bragging. That'll be a celebration day when you can bring the stork to this house."

Alf stepped into the avenue and put his arm around her and pulled her and Frankie close to him.

"You're never too old to learn," he laughed, "so they say."

"Ah, and they also say 'you can't teach an old dog new tricks', don't they, Frankie."

"Grandpa shoot the bogger," enthused Frankie.

Maisie laughed again, put him down and said, "Don't you let your mam hear you. Now then, let's see if we can find some chocolate. Your new brother's name is Alex."

"Alley," repeated Frankie, just before he shoved two squares of Fry's chocolate into his mouth.

★ ★ ★ ★ ★ ★

"I'll be off then, Maisie." Alf put on his coat and tilted his cap. "I'm caddying for Mr. Clements this afternoon so I should get a good tip. I'll take you to the Oak for a drink tonight if I make a few shillings. We'll celebrate your Vera's new baby." He tousled both the boys' hair then set off up Chesil Avenue towards Wollaton Park.

Maisie hung her coat on one of the hooks at the bottom of the stairs, rolled up the sleeves of her blouse and looked all around her.

Alf was quite a good husband as husbands go she always thought, but he was a very untidy man. Pots left in the sink for her to wash; slippers kicked off carelessly lolling against the sideboard; brush-and-comb-set left on top of the sideboard; cut-throat razor, shaving-brush and cream left on the window-sill; Players navy-cut tobacco tin with the lid off and the lid missing as usual. His presence was felt all over the house....it reminded her of a game she had played when she was a little girl....clues left everywhere....a kind of Alfred's hunt-the-slipper. Still, it had been thoughtful of him to see to his own dinner and that of the boys. She could have married a lot worse than Alf.

Maisie was in the middle of washing the pots when a voice called out, "Yoo-hoo....are you there, Maisie? It's only me."

"Hello Nellie, come on in, duck. I've got our Vera's kiddies for the day, come and sit yer down."

Nellie was thin....a gaunt thin, with eyes that seemed too big for their sockets. Her face had a perpetual worried look as though someone had just threatened her life.

The Germans had blown her man to smithereens, but not before he had fathered four children for her to raise and worry herself sick about.

Nellie took in washing and ironing and scrubbed and polished for anyone who could afford to pay her a few shillings. Her hands, forever in soap suds and continuously grasping irons, scrubbing-brushes and dusters were red, swollen and chapped, like ugly pieces of meat cut from some animal's carcass.

Always poor, always hungry, Nellie had never been known to waste anything. She was known to all her neighbours as Mrs. Tealeaf because of the habit she had of draining her teacup when given a cup of tea, drinking the tea-leaves as well, unless she was having her fortune read, then she left a few leaves in the bottom of her cup. "The Pekoe-tips man's on his way round, Maisie." Nellie sat down on a wooden straight-backed chair which was placed just inside the doorway. "I owe him fourpence from last week so I won't have a packet today. Mrs. Cooke didn't send me any ironing yesterday so that's half-a-crown I'm short this week."

"You can borrow a packet of tea from me if you want, Nell. Give it back when you get straight. My lady's having another do on Saturday night so I might be able to get a few bits out. Trouble is though, that Mrs. Guest marks everything with a piece of chalk. All the drink....even the half empty packets of tea and the bottles of coffee. Anybody'd think it was her food the way she guards it, wouldn't they!"

"I pinched a piece of cake from my doctor's house but it was a bit stale," Nellie looked mournful as though she had been robbed of something very special.

"Lets have a nice cup of tea, Nell. Now't like tea to cheer you up." Maisie placed the kettle on the hob and poked at the coal with a highly polished brass poker. "It's enough to make you weep the way the posh folk hang on to everything. Sometimes *I* even have to come home empty handed." Nellie tut-tutted and her sad eyes displayed the agony she felt at Maisie's predicament.

"All that hard work you do for the Carters you'd think they'd be glad to give you a bit o' summat extra. It serves them right if you pinch one or two bits now and then."

Maisie cut two thick slices of bread and lifted the toasting fork off its hook at the side of the hearth.

"Fancy a piece of toast with your tea, Nell? I'm going to have a bit. I'll be glad of a sit down and a natter. I haven't had five minutes since I woke up. Oh, I forget to tell you, duck....our Vera's had another lad." The kettle began to sing its nearly boiling song. "And he's a right pudding 'an all. She's got to have stitches this afternoon."

Nellie folded thin arms across flat chest and hugged herself as though in pain.

"Oh dear....stitches! I had to have stitches when I had my second and they went the wrong road. I reckon it was the doctor's fault — I think he had his training on mailbags, I do."

Maisie poured boiling water into a large brown teapot edged with a band of yellow and shrieked with laughter. "Mailbags....! you're a scream you are, Nell. What did he use for a needle then....a crocherrin' hook! Ey, that reminds me, will you crochèrr some clothes for the baby? They were lovely, those pods and little mittens you did the last time. Do them in blue again, Nell and I'll pay you the same as before. I'll get the wool from the baby shop tomorrow 'cause Alf's caddying this afternoon — be bringing in a few shillings extra."

For the first time since she had entered the house Nellie looked happy. Here was a chance to earn some money. A few shillings to buy food and perhaps some little luxury like a slab of shop cake. The thought of sitting for hours and hours, until late in the evening, fingers aching and sore, did not dismay or depress her. All she could see was the extra money the baby clothes would bring in.

Maisie buttered the toast and handed a slice to Nellie, who licked at the melting butter like a cat, before taking a bite out of the crust.

"How are your two elder lads going on, Nell?" Maisie sat down and sighed the sigh of the grateful. "Do they still send you a few shillings now and then?"Nellie licked butter from her fingers and answered, "They help out when they can but they don't get much, not with being apprentices. But the main thing is they have a roof over their heads and seem to get enough food. Our Tim's leaving school at Christmas and he's staying in Nottingham with me and Ralph. He's going to try and get on at the Raleigh as an apprentice in the Polishing-Shop. It'll be good money when he's twentyone."

"Afternoon ladies, lovely day isn't it!" A cheerful faced man, order book underneath his arm stepped inside the room. "Just mashed I see. That's right, duck....keep me in a job."

"Hello, Mr. Davenport," Maisie gestured towards an easy chair, "sit you down."

"How many packets would you like today, Mrs. Croft? And how about trying the Orange-Pekoe for a change, it's what all them princes in India drink."

"Ooh-ah," Maisie chuckled, "and them Indian princes can afford to chuck their money about an' all can't they! I'll have half-a-pound of the flowered as usual, Mr. Davenport, and can I settle up with you next week?" Maisie took a cup and saucer from the sideboard cupboard and poured the salesman a cup of tea. "I'll straighten up next week if that's all right with you, duck!"

"Right you are then, Mrs. Croft." He scribbled in his order book then put it down on top of the gramophone cabinet. "Would you mind if I had a smoke, ladies?" He fumbled in his pocket and produced a crumpled packet of Woodbines. "I've nearly finished for the day....just got three more calls at the Cottages then I can scram off home. I'm taking the missis to the pictures tonight."

Maisie opened the bottom draw of the sideboard and took out a packet of Players "Medium" cigarettes — she offered them to the salesman.

"Have one of these with your cup of tea. Our Vera's husband gave them to my Alf months ago but he prefers to suck on his mucky pipe. Go on, take them all, we're in a celebrating mood today, our Vera's had another little lad."

"Thank you very much, Mrs. Croft. Your Vera's had another lad then! That's three altogether then, isn't it! Give her my very best wishes and tell her I don't know how she does it. I'd love a little lad," he shrugged his shoulders then looked embarrassed as though he had revealed too much, "wife can't have children you know." He puffed at his cigarette as though trying to hide himself in a screen of smoke. "Still....I suppose it's just as well. Can't afford to have children nowdays can you! Takes me all my time to pay my way as it is."

"Ey up," Maisie cocked her head to one side, "our Frankie's quiet up there.

I'd better nip upstairs and see what he's up to. Dougie's never any trouble. He spends nearly all day asleep in his pram." Maisie poured herself another cup of tea then decided to sit down again. "I'll go up in a minute."

If the scene could have been frozen — like an artist's painting — frozen for future generations to see, maybe they would have been impressed with how serene and contented all the characters looked. How could future generations have possibly imagined the truth from such a painting!

There was Maisie, drinking tea and looking like the lady-of-the-manor, but with no money to pay her tea bill. And Nellie, chewing daintily on her tea-leaves; and her thin beautiful face like that of a Pre-Raphaelite lady, but with the hands of a workhouse-woman, and a stomach that was always hungry.

And then there was the Pekoe-tips salesman, puffing on his cigarette so casually, head resting on the back of the easy-chair, but with a mind frantic with worry because he could never get his books to balance on account of the poverty of his customers. And with a heavy heart mourning the sons he would never have.

For a few seconds the scene *was* frozen and the grandfather clock in the corner at the foot of the stairs ticked the silent moments away; tucked them into the folds of history. Nineteen thirty....nineteen thirty....the pendulum did its stately dance....the dance that no human being could refuse to take part in....the dance of swiftly passing time.

Maisie stood up and walked to the bottom of the stairs; no words were spoken but Nellie, and Bill Davenport, recognised her gentle signal of dismissal.

"I'd better get going then, ladies," Bill reached for his order book. "Settle up next week then, Mrs. Croft, I'll see you next Thursday." He was gone, leaving the lingering smell of cigarette smoke as evidence of his presence.

"I'll sort a few nice patterns out, Maisie. You get the wool then and I'll do you some pram-sets that'll make the little lad look real posh," Nellie plucked at her pinafore with red swollen fingers and added for no particular reason, "It'll soon be Goose-fair won't it!" She stood up ready to go.

"Yes, won't be long, Nell," Maisie answered her before creeping quietly up the stairs to see what mischief Frankie had been up to.

★ ★ ★ ★ ★ ★ ★ ★ ★ ★ ★

CHAPTER THREE

Jack stared at the cigarettes as they went spinning first to the left and then back to the right before bouncing along the chute into the boxes below. The cigarettes reminded him of miniature dancers in some weird ballet. He hated working inside the factory and the sickly aroma of tobacco seemed to him to have been the only thing he could ever remember smelling.

Everyone said working with tobacco is bad for your chest and sometimes he felt an awful panic as he imagined layers of dust coating his lungs, destroying the delicate organs. At the first sign of a cough he would despair and tell himself that he had at last caught the dreaded T.B. that everyone at the factory also feared they would catch. But there was no escaping since being married. Getting a job was difficult — and having a position at the tobacco factory was special — he could not afford to work anywhere else. Three pounds three shillings and a bonus every March that amounted to sixteen per cent of his wages. Vera needed the bonus for clothes and all those extras, and now another baby had come along....well that was it....that was bloody well it!

When Jack had first married Vera he had told her about his wish to go into business on his own and she had agreed with him, been ready to support him. But she had changed her mind after the first baby had been born and seemed to treat him as some sort of imbecile when he had talked about giving up his job and starting something of his own. The job at the cigarette factory was secure, business was booming, especially since the war had ended, and there were no signs of it ever being otherwise. Even women smoked nowadays, and some of them were now being brazen enough to smoke in public. The war had a lot to answer for, he thought sadly, and wished half-heartedly that the firm would go bankrupt — then he would have a chance to escape from the noise and the cloying smell.

Jack sighed deeply and looked round the room at the rest of the workers. They seemed to look happy enough — did not appear to resent the oppressive atmosphere and the sickly stench of tobacco. He tightened a screw on the machine and pushed a wayward cigarette into line; he wished his life away as he thought of tomorrow. Tomorrow was Friday, then it would be weekend again. No more work after 12-0 o'clock on Saturday. If it was fine, he decided to take the boys down to the River Trent for a bit of a picnic. Give Vera a chance to have some peace and quiet, he mused. The thought of Vera with the new baby made him sigh again. She would be a bit edgy for the next few weeks. But he knew how to handle her by now — he would do what he always did — touch her all the time, reassure her of her femininity and allure. It was a rotten time for women when they'd just given birth. All that weight they'd been carrying around; the discomfort; everything swelling....the awful, ugly swelling. He had to pretend like hell when he touched her. And he did not really enjoy making love to her — not after the baby and everything. He always waited the customary six weeks or so; but since the babies, their lovemaking had never seemed the same, not like at first. But he had to pretend, because he knew that was what Vera expected of him; he had to try and make her feel desirable again. But the pleasure had gone out of it somehow — and no sooner had she reverted back to her slender self — then the whole grotèsque business had started all over again. The sickness in the mornings and the awful swelling starting up again. But a man has his needs and things just seemed to happen.

Sometimes, and just lately more often, Jack wished that he had never got married....the whole damn business was too depressing, he thought, more and more. He felt trapped — caught like a badger or a rabbit in a trap.

"I'm trapped in this bloody, awful factory and trapped in that bloody, awful terrace house," he murmered to himself.

"Did you say something, Jack? What's up with you then, duck? You do look miserable today." A pretty girl seated at the opposite side of the machine grinned across at him. "Baby's all right, isn't it?"

"Oh yes thank you, nothing wrong with him. He's a right whopper, biggest one of the lot." He smiled back at her and the gaiety from his carefree days automatically bubbled up to the surface, making him look years younger.

"I was miles away, Iris....miles and miles away. I wish the tea-bell'd go, can't spit a tanner this morning. And I'm tired out as well....Vera started in labour at half-past seven last night so we've all been up since then. He took his time this one did."

He tapped on the side of the machine with his screwdriver and looked irritable.

A coarse faced woman with discontentment etched forever on her tight mouth looked up at him from the cigarette ballet and said, "Didn't bother you much when you were up half the night making him did it! You bleddy men are all the same. You want your fun but you don't want the responsibility that comes with it. You're all the bleddy same you are."

"Oh, don't be so awful Bette. He looks worn out. And you can't stop human nature now can you! He's only human aren't you, Jack? He's only normal."

Jack nodded, reassuring her that he was only normal but he felt so tired he really couldn't have cared less whether they thought he was normal or not. All he wanted was to be left alone to think about his escape from the smell and noise and stupid prattle of the girls. But Bette would not let go.

"You wait 'til you're as old as I am, me duck. Then you tell me how normal it is. Men think about now't else, they don't. You listen to me Iris, and keep yourself to yourself. I only let my Arthur have a bit on Friday pay-day and that's his lot. I don't want houseful of kids. I'll tell you this much....if you're too soft with them they bogger off with some young bit of stuff after they've gev you houseful of kids." She looked meaningfully at Jack and Iris, sniffed loudly, and commenced poking at the jiggling cigarettes.

Jack tried to imagine any man making love to Bette and the thought of it filled him with nausea. A woman with nothing inside of her — giving her body as though part of some ritual that had to be performed once a week to pacify a pagan God. He imagined her talking during the love act....the coarse voice jarring the brain....automatic movements, stifling all real desire....and felt so sorry for her husband, it hurt to think about him even though they had never met.

He looked across the machine at Iris and smiled — Iris returned his smile and hummed a little tune to herself. Jack thought how pretty she looked. He wondered if Iris was a virgin....now he thought about how thirsty he was. Then he wondered again if Iris was still pure and thought about what Bette had said about keeping yourself to yourself. The more he thought about it the more interested he became. He had never thought about Iris in *that* way before — not until Bette had intimated that he had and planted the idea inside the fantasy section of his mind. His imagination took off on its erotic journey and he began to wonder what Iris would look like undressed.

He imagined fondling her breasts, young breasts firm and rounded. She would protest and fight him off of course but he would persist....all women like a man to persist, use a bit of force, they struggled harder but it all added to the excitement.

Now he imagined pinning her down on a bed covered with black satin sheets. He had once seen a picture where the film-star had been lying on a bed covered with black satin-sheets and she had seemed so marble white, so innocent until the villain had forced himself on her and ravished her against her will, that the scene had remained in Jack's mind for days afterwards — it returned to him again as clear as a freshly polished window-pane.

He could picture Iris recumbent on black satin, mouth pouting, half open. Jack could see it all now....the delicate white skin and the inviting mouth.

Yeeeeeoooooowwwww! The tea-bell saved Iris's honour....just in time.

★ ★ ★ ★ ★ ★

Jack sipped at his cup of tea and looked round the canteen at the bustling, queueing, talking, laughing fellow workers. They seemed to him quite happy with their repetitive, boring jobs and their predictable, humdrum lives. Eight o'clock start....six o'clock finish, that was the pattern of their lives, with an hour or two in the pub at the weekends and the apex of the week, an afternoon at the football match, cheering on Forest or County. He supposed it was a big improvement on the old days though....the days his father used to tell him about when people worked far longer hours for a lot less pay.

A giggle of girls fluttered up to his table and surrounded him with smiles and silliness.

What do they store inside their heads thought Jack as he smiled back at them and moved his chair to make more room. Can they really be happy just sitting staring at cigarettes all day long! No....they were just filling in time until they embarked on the adventure of marriage. That was what they all wanted from life — a house of their own filled with fancy furniture and worthless nick-nacks — and a baby to play at house with. They could not possibly be content to sit at a machine all their lives, they'd all go insane. Jack tried to concentrate on the conversation at the table but his mind kept returning to the problem of the girl automatons. The awful part, Jack decided, was that the other workers accepted it, did not feel trapped the same as he did, but the thought repeatedly returned to his mind that there was something very abnormal about sitting at a machine all day long.

I will escape....I will! Jack wanted to cry out and tell everyone to escape with him. But where would they escape to! They were all trapped like the badgers and rabbits.

"You've been at it again then, Jack!" A young girl performed the magnificent feat of talking with a cigarette dangling from the corner of her mouth. Jack watched fascinated as it bobbed up and down as she spoke to him again, "You ought to know what's causing it by now you know."

Jack managed a faint smile and then, for some unexplicable reason, imagined he could hear a river nearby....fast flowing and gushing persistently. The rhythm of the rushing water grew louder as though washing over huge rocks.

"Are you sure you haven't caught T.B., Jack?" The cigarette seemed to be asking him the question. "My mam says that T.B. makes you sexy." Her friends joined in the fun and laughed at the idea of Jack having T.B. The cigarette wagged at him accusingly, "Two men in the stripping department have gone down with it."

The fast flowing river inside Jack's head had now become a swirling torrent. He heard himself laugh with the rest of them but again he wanted to cry out. He was snared like an animal — caught and trapped by circumstances of fate. He decided that he would try and do something about it. His life was precious, a sacred thing that had to be consistently nurtured on dreams and adventure.

The tea-bell announced the end of the brief respite and Jack heaved himself out of the chair and back to reality.

The river inside Jack's head subsided to a gentle murmuring but the feeling of being trapped was even more acute. He did not know how he would eventually escape; only knew that he had to make an effort even if it meant losing his good wage. Over three pounds a week, without overtime, and sixteen per cent bonus on top of that every March. The bonus came in very handy for clothes and a few extras that Vera always needed but he reasoned that if he could start up a business of his own he could earn much more than his wage and the bonus put together. A more rational man would have seen the pitfalls far more clearly than Jack, but Jack was not a rational man. To start with Jack did not have a bank account. New businesses need capital, collateral, contacts; and ruthlessness and an iron nerve. Jack had neither money, iron nerve nor a ruthless streak; only his hatred of being cooped up in the factory spurring him on.

A bit of luck is all I need to start me going, he thought. You can conquer the world with luck on your side. You may just as well be six-foot-under if you're born without luck.

He smiled to himself and gently tapped another wayward cigarette into line.

★ ★ ★ ★ ★ ★ ★ ★ ★ ★ ★ ★

CHAPTER FOUR

Autumn stopped clinging to her cloak of red and gold and discarded it for a lacework shawl of shimmering frost and swirling mists. The days were earlier in welcoming darkness and the gas-lamps sent out their armies of flickering shadows up and down the Radford streets.

Vera closed the door separating the front parlour from the living-room because washday always steamed everywhere up and she wanted to protect the 'best' furniture from blue gloom. It would still take ages to pay for the furniture so she did not want it spoiling.

Jack always lit a fire in the front parlour when it was cold on a Sunday afternoon and later on, when the children had been tucked up in bed, she and Jack shared a jug of beer from the pub and played the wind-up gramophone and pretended they were young again and carefree.

Vera lit the gas under the copper and dragged the dolly-tub out from underneath the sink. The ponch was all set to give the clothes a good bashing and the iron mangle waited to squeeze them in its rollers. Vera opened a new packet of Electrozone and placed a Recketts' blue bag on an old cracked saucer then she sorted the whites from the coloureds and placed them in little heaps on the red tiled floor.

"Are you there?" A woman's voice drifted in through the half open back door.

"Come in," Vera answered automatically as most of the Radford women usually did; hospitality natural to them; a normal reaction.

A swarthy skinned woman smiled at Vera. Black hair plaited and coiled on the top of her head, gold ear-rings dangling, dark eyes penetrating.

"Buy some clothes-peg, missis? Seeing as it's washday I'll bet you could do with a few more pegs. I've made them myself, missis. They'll last forever."

Vera felt irritable — she could have used more pegs but had no money to spare — only enough to buy sausages and a few onions and potatoes. Tomorrow she would be borrowing a few shillings from her mother again, providing Maisie had any to lend.

"Not today thank you," Vera smiled pleasantly, placed one hand on the door latch, and wiped the other one dry on the front of her pinafore.

"Some nice lace then! You're a very pretty lady, I bet you could use some nice lace. You've got a very lucky face, missis. Cross my palm with silver and I'll tell your fortune."

"I haven't got any silver," Vera pushed at the door ever so slightly.

"A silver joey, missis. I'll tell your fortune for a silver joey."

"I've just told you, I haven't got any silver. I haven't got any money at all. I've got three little 'uns and with Christmas nearly here I'm finding things very hard at the moment. Excuse me, but I must get on with my washing, love. I've all the washing to do and my copper's boiling."

The gipsy turned off her obsequious smile as though at the click of a switch then just as quickly turned it back on again.

"I've got little 'uns as well, missis, and I have to tramp the streets in the freezing cold. Find us a couple of pennies then and I'll give you a sprig of lucky dried heather."

"Heather!," Vera scoffed, "in the middle of winter! You ought to be selling Christmas trees, duck, this time of year. And a heath full of heather couldn't bring me any luck not the way my life is at the moment."

"You've got good humour, missis. You're going to be very lucky, you'll see. Let me see your palm and I'll tell you what I can see in the future." She reached for Vera's hand and held onto it. "I've done the palms of royalty."

"Sod off!" Vera snapped at her and pulled her hand away from the gipsy's. The words were out before Vera realised what she was saying.

The gipsy's eyes almost disappeared as they flashed a warning, then she bent down and spat on the door-step. "Bad luck," she told the astonished Vera. "Bad luck all your life and a curse on your last born."

Vera closed the door on the gipsy and on the bad luck omen glistening on the door-step.

"Rubbish," she said out aloud, "absolute tripe." But she hurried through to the kitchen and checked to see if Alexander Joseph was still all right; hemmed in by large stuffed cushions on the sofa in front of the fire.

Alexander gurgled up at her and did a tap-dance lying down, then his chubby hands reached out for her hair which dangled over him in waves and curls.

Nothing wrong with him, and the other two boys were safe with Maisie seeing as it was washday. Every Monday, Maisie collected the boys and took them back to her house and in return Vera did some washing for her mother.

Vera dipped a ladle into the boiling water in the copper and swilled the water over the back door-step where the gipsy had spat then she placed the whites in the copper and added the Electrozone. She took hold of the ponch and bashed the coloureds with all her might getting up a steady rhythm which helped to relieve the tension that had enveloped her body since the episode with the gipsy. She placed the coloureds in a bowl in the sink and then put Jack's overalls in the dolly-tub and commenced with more strenuous bashing. Perspiration trickled down her cheeks and nose and sweat marks appeared under her armpits, staining her jumper, spreading like the outlines of a map.

After fifteen minutes Vera lifted the steaming clothes from the copper and placed them in the clean water which she had ladled into the dolly-tub to which a Recketts' blue bag had been added. More strenuous ponching and the clothes were then ready to go through the mangle.

Vera was proud of her washing and loved to see it in full sail waiving over the back garden, flapping over the few shrubs and flower-beds that Jack had painstakingly set out when they had first moved to Independent Street.

She wiped down the mangle and emptied the water from the dolly-tub down the sink after first pouring some of the water into a bucket to save for washing the scullery floor. The scullery floor had red stone tiles and Vera liked to scrub the tiles until they gleamed, every washday.

After she had tidied the scullery and put everything back into place, Vera took a bottle of Camp coffee from out of the scullery cupboard and made herself a drink. The bottle had been smuggled out of the bank manager's house by Maisie some weeks ago and was used very sparingly by Vera who made do with half a teaspoonful of coffee in her cup of water and dash of milk.

A weak sun thrust itself through the grey skies and Vera felt more cheerful. The feeling of gloom which had surrounded her ever since the encounter with the gipsy began to drift away. Her beautifully clean washing would soon be ready for ironing and the cup of coffee had given her a feeling of well-being. She picked up Alexander and smothered his face and neck with kisses. Alexander clung tightly to her hair and bounced up-and-down in her arms.

"You're not going to have any bad luck, are you!" Vera stroked his head. "No, they can't put a curse on my Alex." She dismissed the tight feeling in her stomach and went into the scullery to make herself a piece of toast.

★ ★ ★ ★ ★ ★

"Yoohoo, are you there, Vera! It's mam." Maisie called out as she returned with Frankie and Douglas. "It's a nice drying day, duck. Did you get that stain out of Alfie's best shirt?"

"Put the kettle on, mam," Vera called back to her from upstairs. "I'm just making the beds, be down in a minute. Yes, I got the stain out, but I had to scrub at it first with the nail brush."

After a few minutes Vera walked down the stairs holding a chamber-pot in either hand; small white one which Frankie used; large pale blue one with red roses painted on the bottom for Jack and herself.

"I'm just going to empty the poes, mam." Vera emptied the contents of the chamber-pots into a bucket then hurried down the garden path to the lavatory. When she returned she rinsed the pots under the tap in the kitchen sink and added a few drops of Pine disinfectant in each one.

"A gipsy gave me bad luck this morning, mam." Vera sat down on the sofa at the side of Alexander and pushed back straggling hair which tickled her face — her hair had lost most of its curl because of the steam from the copper and the damp atmosphere. "She said I would have bad luck and she put a curse on Alex. Isn't she evil....how could anyone put a curse on an innocent child!"

"Oh, you don't want to take any notice of that, duck. They're no different to you and me, now are they! How can they put a curse on anybody, I ask you! Don't be so daft, our Vera."

"It's just a funny feeling I've got," Vera shrugged her shoulders. "She spit on the back door-step and looked ever so vicious," Vera forced a giggle and continued, "I swilled the step with boiling water."

"Ha-ha-ha....you daft thing....you should have chucked a bucket over her the dirty scrounger." Maisie lifted Dougie from out of his pram and felt at his nappie. "You're all wet aren't you, love. Let gramarr change him then. I'll tell you this much, Vera. She'd better not let me see her round here."

"She said she'd done the palms of royalty."

"What! Palm trees! They're about the only palms she's looked at. Now then, drink your tea and I'll have a look at your leaves. That's the only way to tell fortunes. Grandma used to read the leaves and I wish I had a florin for every time she was right. I take after her you know. Me mam said I was the spittin' image of her. 'Specially round the eyes she said."

Maisie smiled at Dougie....contented now that his nappie had been changed....he was eating a biscuit and showering himself and his pram with crumbs.

"You are enjoying that aren't you, me duck. A nice custard cream your gramarr got from her lady's house for you. Look at him Vera....he looks just like your dad when he smiles. He's going to be a real Parkinson. I can't see any of your Jack in him, can you? He don't look anything like a Denbey."

"She said I would have bad luck all the rest of my life and she cursed my last born," Vera spoke softly as though repeating lines from some tragic Greek play. "It made me feel ever so funny."

"Pass us your cup and stop being so daft."

Vera tipped the remainder of the tea into a saucer and peered at the tea leaves then she handed the cup to Maisie.

"I can see a river all down the side here," Maisie tilted the cup. "It's definitely a river....it goes up-and-down just as though it's flowing along. I'll bet you're going somewhere really nice. It'll be a day-trip to Colwick on one of the pleasure boats. You'll be going for a lovely day out to Colwick. And I can see a big crowd here, all gathered round two objects. Can't make out what the objects are, but they're right in the centre of the crowd. It looks like some sort of celebration," she tilted the cup to the right and added, "another two here as well. Two very distinct shapes that look almost identical. They've got tails by the looks of it. Yes....it's definitely tails. It looks like two horses, Vera! I'll bet your Jack's going to get a double up at the bookies. Does he have a crafty bet, Vera? I bet he does on the quiet. They all like a little flutter don't they, so that they can dream what they'd do with the money if they had a big win!" Maisie placed the cup back in its saucer. "There you are, nothing but nice things. A lovely day out at Colwick and a bit of a win on the horses for Jack. That gipsy wants to use some Panshine on her crystal-ball. She's got the future all clouded up."

Vera laughed with her mother but she still could not get rid of the uneasy feeling which seemed to thread in-and-out of her chest like ice cold threads of wool.

★★★★★★★★★★★

CHAPTER FIVE

"Jack....I think I'm pregnant again!" Vera stepped inside the bedroom and delivered the news along with Jack's early morning tea and Sunday newspaper.

The cry which escaped half strangled from Jack's throat first of all made the hair at the nape of her neck tingle and then had her stomach churning with anger.

"Well it's your fault....no use making that row!" Vera threw the newspaper onto the end of the bed. She rubbed her fingers through her sleep tangled hair and had an irresistible urge to tear it out by the roots. She stood transfixed — staring into Jack's eyes as though trying to drag out a solution from the brain behind them.

"You can't be....Oh my God you can't be....! I've been careful....! you know I've been careful!" Jack gulped at the tea not caring whether it burned his mouth; not caring about anything.

"It was that Sunday." Vera could feel the strength flowing out of her; naming the day; pinpointing the hour; the minute: the very second it had happened, stamped it with the seal of finality. She imagined the child lying asleep — arms folded across its chest — a smug smile on its lips — safely anchored inside her womb. A tadpole with its shape, colour, sex.... everything that it would be throughout its life already patterned and shaped in miniature, safe inside her body.

"Can't you get something to get rid of it?" Jack slumped against the pillows, "what was it that woman at the clinic told you about?"

"Slippery Elm," Vera said the words gently and thought how nice they sounded. Slippery Elm....it reminded her of a beautiful tree with whispering leaves and moisture glistening all over the trunk and branches. "But it's very dangerous. I'm nearly two months gone, I don't think I dare try anything like that. I didn't tell you before because I didn't want to worry you. I didn't think I could be, I thought it was because of the baby, everything settling down again. But I've started being sick in the mornings again so now I know for sure. I told you to be careful, Jack: I told you again and again."

"As though I haven't got enough to worry about with Christmas here as well." Jack banged the cup-and-saucer down on top of the bedside cabinet and got out of bed. "I'm getting up....some chance of enjoying my only morning lie-in now. Bleddy hell....what a damned bleddy awful life....!"

Vera turned to leave the bedroom but at the door paused and said, "You will never make love to me again, Jack. I hope you're listening to me because I mean every word I say."

"It won't bother me," Jack pulled on his trousers. "I'm fed up with making love to a zombie." He put his slippers on. "So you needn't start any of your blackmailing, because I've had enough. Enough of you; marriage; bleddy job; in fact, of being alive!"

"It has nothing to do with blackmailing you, Jack. And while we're on the subject," she paused and breathed in deeply before adding solemnly, "I hate it. I've always hated it....you mauling me and using me. It's disgusting and degrading all that mauling when I've just had a baby....you make me feel filthy. I don't care what you do or who with....just so long as you leave me alone. And I won't have this baby — I'll get rid of it even if it kills us both." She shuddered as though she had just seen something repulsive. "The whole business is absolutely disgusting and I'm glad I've told you."

"I agree." Jack's face was grey; he felt so desolate it was as though his soul had deserted his body and because of it his eyes were incapable of mirroring any feeling; they stared at the hateful world, unseeing, uncomprehending. The river inside his head flowed through the canals of his brain and it seemed as though all the trapped animals in the world were crying out simultaneously in sympathy with his agony. "I quite agree with you, Vera. And I wish to God that I had never laid eyes on you."

"Santa's coming tonight in't he, Dad?" Frankie peeped round the bedroom door. Vera put her hand on his shoulder and forced a smile to blossom on her agonised face.

"Yes and I wonder what he'll bring you, Frankie! I'll bet he'll bring you some lovely things. His bag'll be bulging with toys when he comes down the chimney. He'll bring you a painting-box and some colouring-books and a jigsaw and a sugar-pig."

"And a few more nails for my coffin," murmured Jack.

Vera took hold of Frankie's hand and led him down the stairs away from Jack's anger.

Jack sat down on the edge of the bed and stared in to the dressing table mirror. A sad-eyed, despairing image gazed sympathetically back at him. He leaned forward towards his image and tried to see inside himself — as though seeking an answer from the sad shadow that stared back at him so full of tangled complexity and unhappiness.

Suddenly, Jack began to cry. Softly at first then in painful half held-in sobs. The more he looked at his reflection the more he cried. Back....back he went in his mind, over the years he had frittered away. He was a little boy again; it was all right to cry when you were a little boy; nobody thought it strange then. You were comforted and cuddled when you were a child. Jack cried for the comforting arms of his frail consumptive mother who was now lying in Lenton churchyard.

He cried for the safety of his father's lap, his dear father who had taught him to read, played silly games with him, until the pit had crushed the life out of him and who would now lie forever in darkness as though still at work in the black bowels of Radford pit.

"Mam....dad....!" he implored them, but they remained silent....trapped in the blackness.

Jack put his head in his hands and vowed to himself that this would be the very last time he would cry; about anything: anything at all that God chose to hammer him with.

He walked downstairs ready to face the spirit of Christmas.

★★★★★★★★★★★★

CHAPTER SIX

"Christians awake....salute the happy morn....whereon the saviour of mankind was born." The sweet music of the Salvation Army band floated down Independent street sending its goodwill message into every home.

Vera poked at the bacon crackling in the fryingpan then cut slices of bread and stacked them onto a plate.

Jack was working half-heartedly on a jigsaw puzzle which was proving to be quite difficult because it was a picture of soldiers in the middle of a battle and there was a lot of dark grey sky and the pieces all looked the same.

Frankie was painting in a colouring-book and Dougie's cheeks were bulging with the remainder of a sugar-pig whilst he cuddled a teddy-bear which squeaked everytime he pressed its belly. Alexander slept, oblivious to his first Christmas.

"Come on, get your breakfasts." Vera put the bacon and eggs onto the plates and made a fried-egg sandwich for Dougie.

"Where's yours?" Jack reached for the sauce bottle. "Aren't you having any breakfast?"

"Can't face any food," Vera's face had the look of a martyr. "I could be sick again just looking at food....just smelling it turns my stomach over."

Jack dipped a piece of fried-bread in the tomato-juice and pretended not to hear.

"Hark at the Salvation Army. They're doing 'See amid the winter snow' now. I wonder if it will snow later on? It's cold enough in't it! If it snows we'll make a great big snowman in the garden and put one of my scarves round his neck to keep him warm."

The boys laughed and looked out of the window, peering into the sky, willing it to snow. It was a happy scene on the surface but the tension between Vera and Jack smouldered like a slowly awakening cancer.

After breakfast Vera washed the pots and tidied the kitchen, then she cut a thick slice of bread, crumbled it on the bread-board and added parsley and thyme and salt and pepper, then the mixture was left to stand.

The chicken which the family were having for Christmas dinner was already slowly roasting in the oven.

"I'll light the fire in the front-room for you," Jack took hold of the brass coal-scuttle and stood at the top of the cellar steps, "Be nice and warm by the time we have our dinners."

"Put some more money in the gas-meter, while you're down the cellar,"

Vera called from the scullery, "and in the electric. There's some pennies in the tin at the top of the cupboard if you haven't got enough."

Jack fed the greedy meters at the top of the cellar steps their coppers, then he carried on down into the cellar. The musty smell reminded him of damp clothes drying round a coal-fire, all mingled with the aroma of December-fog.

Jack had whitewashed the cellar walls when he and Vera had first moved into the house but the two rooms still had an eerie look. Coal dust everywhere giving the walls strange patterns and decorated with huge cobwebs that draped themselves in every corner dangling like forgotten Christmas garlands from the ceiling.

The wall dividing the two rooms was of good solid red brick which Jack had not whitewashed. A heap of coal and slack stood in one room and, as Jack disturbed the dust with the dustpan, it danced in the filter of light which shone down from the cellar-grate above. In the other room were tools, half-empty tins of paint, a hobbing-iron, old brass fender, and magazines and newspapers used for lighting the fires.

Jack filled the coal-scuttle with small pieces of coal and some slack and a bundle of sticks which were held together with a piece of twisted wire.

★ ★ ★ ★ ★ ★

The fire, when it had taken hold, transformed the front-room, like a dull looking woman who has just tried on a dazzling ball gown.

Jack helped Frankie to carry the Christmas presents into the front-room and winked at him.

"I wonder what Santa's brought for your mam? He told me he'd put it in here somewhere. Come on, help me to look for it. Perhaps it's in the cupboard over there! Or....it could be behind that chair!"

Frankie's eyes shone with excitement as he hurried from cupboard to sideboard....back from sideboard to cupboard, and then he lay on his stomach peering underneath the three-piece-suite.

Jack opened a drawer in the sideboard and took out a small packet tied with a green satin bow.

"I reckon this must be your mam's present. Go and fetch her, tell her what we've found."

Vera wiped her hands dry down the front of her pinafore and followed Frankie into the front-room. She feigned surprise on seeing the present and opened it very slowly. Shiny, brand new, snug in between folds of cottonwool, was a pearl necklace. Vera looked genuinely surprised as she saw the gift. She lifted the pearls into the air and stroked them lovingly.

"Oh Jack, it's beautiful." She looked like a young, gauche girl and for a few moments her eyes held warmth as they looked into Jack's eyes. Then, back came the anxious dead look that Jack had grown to hate; her back stiffened and her mouth clamped tight then she asked, "But how could you afford it? You can't afford these, Jack."

"Santa brought it," Jack tried to keep his voice steady and added quickly,

"I paid into a Christmas club at work. A bloke who owns a jeweller's on Hyson Green runs the club and his daughter works in our room — she collects the money every week. You've always wanted a pearl necklace....well it's not a real one of course....but you can't tell can you! It'll look lovely with your maroon crêpe dress, the one I bought from Marks & Spencers for your birthday. It'll look real classy."

"I can't get into that, I've put too much weight on and if I'm having another...."

"You'll get into it," Jack interrupted her, "things'll work out all right, love. Now then....let's see how you look in your lovely new pearls."

He placed the necklace around her neck and fastened the clasp. Vera looked at herself in the mirror above the fireplace, patted her hair and plucked at her pinafore.

"They don't look right with my pinny on and my hair all of a mess."

"Can I paint them for you, mam?" Frankie dipped his paint brush into a blob of bright orange paint.

Jack and Vera looked at one another and laughed — for a while the tension between them eased a little.

"We'd better go and see what Santa's brought for your dad hadn't we!" Vera reached for Frankie's hand and led him into the kitchen. "Have a look in the bottom cupboard where we keep all the shoes," she set him on the trail. "Santa whispered down the chimney to me....he said he'd left something for your dad in the shoe cupboard."

Frankie held the paper parcel high in the air.

"I've found it," he rushed back into the front-room, "I've found it, dad!"

"This is a nice pullover," Jack held the present in front of his chest, "I don't know how Santa could afford this." He looked at Vera.

"He must be paying into a diddle-um," Vera answered him. "Do you like the colour, Jack? It'll go with your best suit and it's a lovely soft wool, it'll keep you nice and warm."

"It's the best pullover I've ever had." Jack wrapped it in the paper again and placed it on top of the sideboard. "Now....what do you say to a nice glass of sherry while you're doing the dinner? Just a little one — put some colour in your cheeks."

"I don't think so, Jack, not on an empty stomach."

"Just try a little one — might help to settle your stomach."

"All right then, I'll just have a small one," she conceded. Jack poured sherry into two red coloured wine-glasses which were only washed and used at Christmastime.

"Merry Christmas, Vera."

"Merry Christmas, Jack."

They drank the sherry down — like ill people do when they're taking medicine — as though expecting it to balm the hurt which gripped each of them; cure the misery that flowed through their bodies.

"It's a good sherry, Vera. One thing about being in the grocer's Christmas club, he always puts a good sherry in the hamper."

"So he ought to as well. I spend a fortune with him all the year round. I'd better go and put the pudding on now, it takes ages to steam." She retreated to the scullery once more and commenced bustling about.

"Mam's put some silver joeys in the pudding and I'm going to get one.... I'm going to get one," Frankie chanted over and over and had a go at pressing a brightly painted spinning-top. The clatter woke up Alexander who had been sleeping soundly behind his fortress of stuffed cushions on the sofa in front of the fire — he began to whimper.

Dougie crawled towards the spinning-top attracted by the humming noise and grabbed at it with both hands. Frankie gave him a shove and in a few seconds the room was filled with crying from all three, an out-of-tune dirge sung in triplicate.

Jack knew that he should have concentrated on pacifying the boys, but somehow his thoughts seemed to be fixed on other things. The sherry; pearl necklace; Christmas hamper; pullover; all the furniture: almost everything he looked at had been bought on the never-never. That's what keeps me trapped, he thought bitterly. I'm shackled by all these things. It's not just Vera and the boys — it's the furniture and — it's every bleddy thing you look at.

But you have to have things, you need things, he argued with himself. No you don't, he answered back, all those people who live in Africa and India manage without. And then there were all those Red-Indians....all that lot. Why....they managed with tents and a few pots and pans. They didn't have to have rooms full of furniture; sideboards; dressers; three-piece-suites; gas-stoves as well as an open fire to cook on: they got by all right as far as he knew.

And they had lots of children, but they seemed to cope with large families. His Uncle Bill had gone to India 'fighting and what-have-yer' in 1920, and Egypt in 1923, and he had come back to England with photographs of some of the *blackies* from the villages and he'd said how happy the people were. There had been loads of kids everywhere, swarming all over they were; all grinning and showing lovely white teeth and all the older people were laughing as well and looking happy and contented. They hadn't needed bedroom-suites and Wilton carpets and best Irish linen tablecloths for Sunday teas. They all mucked in together and would have gone on being quite happy with their lot, he reckoned, if the British hadn't gone sticking their big noses in. Because of the bleddy nosy British there were now lots of Indians and Egyptians and Blackies just as trapped as he was. Thinking they needed houses with loads of rooms — rooms crammed full of furniture that they wouldn't use half the time and all bought on the never-never he supposed.

Jack let out a cry when the next thought filled his mind. Why....I'm even paying for my coffin on the never, and Vera's and the boys'. He laughed and Frankie and Dougie stopped crying, curious to know what he was laughing at. Alexander decided to gurgle and tap-dance instead of cry so, once again, bedlam gave way to tranquility.

★ ★ ★ ★ ★ ★

The Christmas dinner filled Vera and Jack 'right up to the top' as they called it and the sherry had produced drowsiness. The two elder boys settled down for their afternoon nap and Alexander fell asleep sucking on a spoonful of sugar which Vera had tied in the corner of a handkerchief.

Jack and Vera each dozed in an armchair and the wireless was switched on — turned down low so that the carols and Christmas songs flowed over the front-room giving out a soothing festive lullaby for the whole of the family.

At half-past three Vera began to prepare the children for the journey down to Maisie's house for the ritual Christmas tea. Nappies were changed on Alexander and Dougie, and Frankie had his hair brushed, teeth cleaned and a warm flannel wiped over his mouth.

By the time half-past four arrived the daylight was turning steely grey and the atmosphere had turned much colder. A stillness had come once again to Radford that was quite different to any other day of the year: as though the inhabitants were holding their breath expecting something to happen; like it had all those hundreds of years ago.

Christmas morning in Radford was filled with children's laughter; church-bells; people calling to one another; dogs barking; bicycle-bells. But by late afternoon the quietness was always there — that reverent stillness.

"Are you putting your new pullover on, Jack?" Vera pressed a wave in at the front of her hair then pushed a grip in to keep it in place. "I've got my pearls on, look!" She turned from the mirror to face him. "They look nice with this grey jumper, don't they! I look like one of those posh women who dine out at the Ritz. Pity the stork's coming again, they would have looked lovely with my Marks & Spencer frock."

"Grandpa's going to shoot the bogger," Frankie heard the word stork.

"You what!" Vera's eyes widened in amazement, Jack hid a grin behind his hand.

"Grandpa's going to shoot the bogger," Frankie repeated seriously.

"Good idea if you ask me," said Jack acting solemn, "I'll buy grandpa some bullets for his gun."

They set off along Dennison street, Vera pushing the pram, Alexander in the pram with Dougie perched on the top and Frankie hand-in-hand with Jack.

They walked down Edinburgh street and then on to Connaught street. As it was so cold Mrs. Cohen was not sitting in her usual place just inside the door but as the family passed her house she waved at them from behind the front-room window.

"Wait there a minute," she mouthed from behind the glass, then hurried to the front-door. "Is this the new baby then?", she peered inside the pram. "Such a lovely boy — you're all lovely boys. Wait and see what I've got for you." She disappeared inside the house then returned clutching a well worn brown leather handbag. She rummaged inside and held up three silver joeys, one for each child. After she had given Dougie and Frankie theirs she then insisted on pressing the remaining coin into one of Alexander's clenched fists.

"He must hold it tight," she forced the coin between the tiny fingers, "must hold it nice and tight then it'll bring him good luck. He'll never be short of money if he squeezes it tight."

"Better let me have one to squeeze then, Mrs. Cohen," Jack joked with her. Mrs. Cohen smiled at him and answered, "Who needs money when there's such lovely children in the house! And all boys....all boys!" She rocked from side-to-side in that peculiar way of hers. "You like some Christmas cake, Mrs. Denbey? Lovely icing-sugar for the children. My Sammy wasn't able to get over to Nottingham to see me and I've so much food to spare."

"No, it's all right thank you, Mrs. Cohen, we've got plenty of food," Vera took hold of the pram handle ready to move on. Mrs. Cohen threw out an invisible net that held them rooted outside her door.

"Won't take a minute. You Frankie....you come with me and I'll put some nice cake in a bag for you. That's it, you come with me, duckie."

They escaped at last but not before Mrs. Cohen had insisted on giving the two elder boys a hug and a kiss.

"Poor old duck," said Jack as they proceeded down Denman street, "her Sammy puts on her don't he! He ought to have come for Christmas." Jack thought about what Mrs. Cohen had said, about his boys, all the way down to Sodom.

"Come on here, let's have you." Maisie ushered the children towards a faded maroon ottoman. "Let's lift you up here out the way and you can tell me what Santa's brought. He forgot to leave all your toys at your house so he brought some parcels here and gave them to grandad Alf. Grandad Alf met him up on Canterbury road and he had twenty rheindeer pulling his sleigh. Grandad counted them as they went by, didn't you, grandad?"

Maisie tugged at the sleeve of Frankie's coat. "Give me your coats and I'll see if I've got a bottle of dandelion and burdoch in my pantry."

"Mrs. Cohen gave us some Christmas cake, mam," Vera handed her coat to Alf and the cake to Maisie. She turned to face Maisie, fingered her pearl necklace.

"What do you reckon to my present then?"

Maisie did not look surprised but instead took a small packet from the sideboard drawer and handed it to Vera.

"These might come in handy," Maisie winked at Jack, "Merry Christmas, love." Vera opened the packet and was delighted with the gift. A pair of clip-on pearl ear-rings — a perfect match to the necklace.

"Been a bit of a conspiracy somewhere along the line," Alf sucked on his pipe and made a popping noise. "Go on then Maisie, give Jack his present now, I know you can't wait."

Jack held the pullover against himself and said, "This is a posh 'un Maisie, thank you very much. It'll go a treat with my sports-coat won't it Vera!"

"I got Nellie Tealeaf to knit it for you, Jack. She's a beautiful knitter." Maisie fished about in the sideboard cupboard, "You and Alf have both had the same 'cept where yours is a green one Alf's is a pale blue one. Now then, where's those other parcels for my lads?" She held the parcels close to her breasts.

"Here you are Frankie, one for you and one for Dougie." She handed the third parcel to Vera, "And this is for little Alex."

There was a dog that squeaked when you pulled it along the floor for Dougie; a large train-engine you could sit in that Alf had made out of some old bits of wood and painted bright red for Frankie; and a beautifully crocheted white shawl for Alexander.

Jack and Vera gave Alf tobacco, and a box of hand-made cigarettes that Jack had bought from the factory and Maisie was thrilled with the crêpe-de-chine blouse with the mother-of-pearl buttons down the front that Vera had bought in a clothing-club from a shop on Denman street.

Jack looked at the smiling faces all around him and felt rather ashamed. Why do I always want more and more out of life, he mused. This is what matters when it's all boiled down. People being kind to one another — loving and giving. I'm loving and giving, he thought, I'm kind to people. Well, perhaps not all the time, but I would be if I had a bit more money....more freedom. Then perhaps I'd feel happy all the time like I do now. Relaxed and safe, not worrying about where the next meal's coming from; about feeding and clothing my family. But I'm never allowed to forget my responsibilities ....it's just as though I've got a tiny bird sitting on my shoulder, whispering in my ear over-and-over again, 'don't forget your responsibilities — don't forget to worry about your family and all those bills today — you must keep on worrying, it's good for you.' If I could be hypnotised....get some bloke to swing a watch on a chain in front of my eyes and say, 'don't worry about anything', I reckon I could muddle through life all right. I wonder if I could find some bloke to hypnotise me!

"Jack....Jack....you look as though you've gone into a trance," Maisie's voice spear-headed into his jungle of thoughts. "I said would you like some pork sandwiches for your tea or I've got some of your favourite, a nice piece of polony. We had a piece of pork for our Christmas dinner and it was lovely, wasn't it, Alf! I bet they could hear us crunching on the crackling, next door. There's plenty left for a nice sandwich, and I've got some pork-pie from my lady's house and loads of mince-pies."

"We didn't have our dinner till three," Alf settled back in his armchair next to the fire. "Maisie went to help with the Christmas dinner at the Carter's house, so we had to wait till she got back. Got a nice drop of port for later on, Jack. Tell 'um what you did, Maisie."

"Well you know the piece of chalk Alf uses to mark the scores when he plays darts with Jim next door! I popped it in my handbag and took it with me to the Carter's and when Mrs. Guest took the turkey through to be carved, I poured some port into a clean Camp coffee bottle, rubbed the chalk mark off the port bottle and put another one on further down."

"Clever in't she!" Alf looked pleased. "They could have done with a few like Maisie at the Army Headquarters during the war. She's more resourceful than any of the doddering 'owd boggers they'd got in charge of things during the Great War."

"Aah, I'd 'ave sorted them out all right. I'd 'ave soon got them off their arses and thought of a way to stop all our men being slaughtered in their thousands. All those lovely young lads blown to smithereens and torn to shreds on the barbed wire." Tears flooded her eyes but Vera did her rescuing act again.

"Ey mam, what do you think to this? You know the people who keep that toffee-shop on Hartley road....? well their youngest girl's run off with one of the foremen out of Jack's room. Jack didn't know, they kept it ever so quiet, but the woman at the fruit-shop told me because her daughter's thick with the girl who's run off."

It did the trick and Maisie's eyes drained of tears as she soaked up the scandal.

"Not young Gloria! The one with that lovely head of red hair! Still, you know what they say....people with red hair are very hot-blooded you know." She buttered bread and cut polony into slices. "My gran used to say never trust a man with red hair or a man who wears a bow-tie."

"Don't be so daft, woman," Alf scoffed, "how can a bow-tie do 'owt?"

"I don't know, I expect it means if a man wears a bow-tie he's a bit smarmy. A bit of a ladies' man and can't be trusted."

"I've never heard 'owt so daft in my life....have you, Jack?" he looked for an ally, "can't be trusted if you wear a bow-tie!"

Jack played safe and replied, "A bow-tie man could be a bit shifty I suppose and I think red haired people are a bit nasty. They're supposed to have fiery tempers....are hell to live with."

"Well I've never heard 'owt so daft in me life," Alf poked at his pipe with a piece of twisted wire.

"I've invited Nellie Tealeaf round for a drink of port and a mince-pie a bit later on," Maisie started on the pork. "Her lads are going round to their pal's house so she'd be on her own. Didn't want her to be on her own at Christmas. Did you know the Pekoe-tips man's a bit sweet on her, Vera?"

Vera was very interested.

"He's not is he! What's he been saying to her then?"

"It's not what he's been saying exactly but...."

"Here we go agin," Alf winked at Jack, "give 'em a bit of a smile and they'll stretch it into a mile of lovemaking and carryings on. I blame the pictures.... all those soppy folk kissing each other and doing....and carrying on."

"Oh, I love a good picture," Maisie cut the sandwiches into dainty squares, "I saw a Mary Pickford picture at the Boulevard last week and I cried my eyes out. It was all about this young girl whose dad was out of work and poorly and this 'ere young girl got mixed up with ever such a bad man who was awful to her."

"He hadn't got red hair, had he?" Alf chuckled.

"I bet he wore a bow-tie," Jack joined in the fun.

"Oh you two....you're always pulling my leg. Anyway, she got some money for her dad, but by the time she did it was too late, her poor dad had died."

"What happened to Mary Pickford then?" Vera looked worried.

"Oh, she ended up with another bloke who she thought was poor but he had been kidding her all along," Maisie explained the plot.

"Now he must definitely have worn a bow-tie," Alf tried to look serious. "Fancy telling lies to poor Mary Pickford."

"I'm not too keen on her," Vera helped herself to a pork sandwich, "I'd sooner have Janet Gaynor."

"I'd rather have Mary Pickford's husband," Maisie sat down at last. "I think Douglas Fairbanks is the handsomest man in the pictures. And all that swashbuckling he does....all that swinging on chandeliers and flying through the air from curtain to curtain. I think he's ever so brave."

"If I swung on your curtains the bloomin' house'd fall down," Alf laughed at her, "and aren't you going to draw them by the way? Everybody'll be gawping in if you don't."

Maisie peered out of the window — the darkness was complete except for the light from the gas-lamps.

"Let's leave them open a bit longer....we can see the stars. I've got a feeling it'll snow a bit later on. If we draw the curtains we won't be able to see it will we, Frankie! And Dougie don't know what snow looks like."

Maisie stayed where she was by the window.

"What yer looking for, Maisie....the star of Bethlehem?" Alf's jovial mood continued. Neither Maisie, Vera nor Jack spoke but all three felt a tingling sensation down their spines, and Jack thought, this is what it's all about: bright stars; snowflakes; goodwill-towards-men: the holy child. He got up from his chair, walked over to Vera and placed his hand on her shoulder.

"Are you feeling all right, love?" he whispered intimately.

"Yes I'm fine, Jack," Vera fingered the pearl necklace at her throat. "Look at Alex, fast alseep again. He's a good little soul isn't he!"

Everyone looked at Alexander and for a few brief moments, a feeling of well-being encapsulated them all in a cocoon of contentment.

★★★★★★★★★★★★

CHAPTER SEVEN

Vera sat on the edge of the bed, looked at herself in the mirror and spoke to her image, "You've got to do it....there's no other way out. You can't go through with all that pain again. The worn out feeling and the awful despair that comes with having another child to feed."

Perspiration glistened on her top lip — even though it was January and icy cold in the bedroom Vera felt a raging heat surging through her body — the heat of fear.

The piece of slippery-elm bark lay on the bed at the side of her. She picked it up with the tips of her fingers and felt faint when the sickly aroma of carbolic soap assaulted her senses. Now, what had the woman she'd met at the clinic said! It was easy — she had done it many times because her husband was continuously out of work and she was always 'falling for a baby'. You wash the piece of bark with carbolic soap and lie back on the bed with your legs wide apart. Then you push the bark up....up into your womb as far as it will go and the heat from your body makes the bark expand. It punctures the protective membrane surrounding the baby and within a few hours the lot comes away. It was all so easy and simple the woman had told her.

Vera pushed at the bark and experienced pain that spiralled up and up until it had travelled into her head and burst like a million needles sticking into her brain.

She lay quietly for a few minutes not daring to move — she turned her head to look at the alarm-clock at the side of the bed — it was nearly three o'clock. Tuesday at three o'clock, the time I murdered my baby, she thought. No.... it wasn't a baby; not a proper baby; not a smiling, gurgling, sleeping, soft, warm, sweet-smelling baby. It was just a lump of flesh, not properly formed. 'Maybe it's a little girl' said a voice hiding somewhere inside her brain. 'You've always wanted a little girl, with ribbons in her hair and pretty dresses.'

You can't make me imagine a shapeless lump of flesh is a little girl, Vera answered the voice back, then she placed her hands on her stomach and rubbed gently from side-to-side. "It's not a little girl in there....it's not....it's not anything....not anything at all....!"

Another look at the time....half-past three and still Vera dare not move. The boys would be waking up from their afternoon nap, there was the tea to prepare, she had to get up.

The slippery-elm bark was firmly lodged inside her body; Vera gently probed with her fingers and gritted her teeth as she caught hold of the bark.

She pulled at the bark but it was difficult to retrieve because her body was tense and the passageway to her womb dry.

I've changed my mind....I've changed my mind....! Vera tugged at the bark again and it came from her body reluctantly.

Oh dear God, please forgive me....I've changed my mind. Please don't let the baby be harmed. I'm sorry, God....don't let the baby be harmed!

She sat up and stared at the bark. Oh thank God, thank God, she murmured over and over again as she examined the bark for tell-tale signs of blood. Perhaps I've damaged the baby somehow! Another thought set her heart racing. Maybe I've damaged the baby somehow, there'll be something awful wrong with it! It'll be deformed! What was it the gipsy said? She searched past memories for the exact words. A curse on my last born, that's what she said. And it'll all come true now. I've damaged my baby, I know I have.

She staggered towards the bedroom door still holding on to the slippery-elm bark. She reached the kitchen and threw the bark onto the fire, then sat hunched in an armchair watching until the flames had devoured and exterminated all traces of the disgusting piece of wood. Her mind was swamped with terrifying thoughts as her imagination unchained itself and soared off in all directions. A child with one arm; one leg; sightless; a crippled withered frame: the torment went on and on until she wished she could have died, right there, huddled in the armchair. Just close my eyes, she thought, and never wake up again.

"I'm hungry, mam," Frankie ran from the bottom of the stairs and climbed onto her lap. "Can I have some bread and jam?"

Vera hugged him and answered, "Let's have a look in the pantry and see what we've got. Wouldn't you like some nice bread and dripping with some black jelly in? I've got a cupful of dripping made from out of grandma's Sunday joint and it's lovely. I could toast you some bread and the dripping will be all runny, just how you like it."

"I like black jelly," Frankie nodded his head solemnly, "and can I hold the toasting-fork, mam?"

"All right then, but don't get too near the fire. Keep the bread away from the bars 'else you'll burn it."

Vera went to the pantry and took out the cup of dripping. She cut slices of bread and stuck the toasting-fork through one slice and handed it to Frankie. I seem to be all right, she thought anxiously, a slight pain in my stomach but nothing drastic.

Vera lathered the slice of toast with dripping and handed it to Frankie. "Let's have a bit of music shall we, Frankie! I'll turn the wireless on and the Childrens' programme'll be on soon, you like that don't you! Now be a good lad and sit there and eat your tea, I'm just going upstairs to get our Dougie."

At five o'clock all the children had been fed and changed. Vera relaxed a little and made herself some toast and a pot of tea. Her stomach felt hard, she rubbed her hands over it again and told herself that everything was still all right. She willed everything to be all right, repeating again-and-again that the

baby was safe; with arms folded tightly across its chest; still smiling and snug
and secure inside the safety of her womb.

★ ★ ★ ★ ★ ★

Jack arrived home from work at ten-past six and was in quite a good mood.
"They want me to do a bit of overtime," he put his slippers on and settled
down in an armchair. "The factory's got an order from overseas so we've got
another deadline to make. It all helps towards the 'bonus', Vera. Should get a
good 'bonus' again this year. He scanned the pictures section of the
Nottingham Evening Post. "There's a Carl Brisson film on at the Elite this
week. If you can get your mam to sit with the boys I'll take you when I get paid
on Friday. I like Carl Brisson, he's a good actor."

Vera went across to the window and looked outside. The row of terraced-
houses running parallel at the bottom of the garden loomed ghostlike below
the dark grey sky. Dotted here and there were lights from kitchen windows.
The scene reminded Vera of a huge ocean liner with lighted portholes,
motionless on a still sea. She tried to imagine what it would be like, sailing
away on a luxury liner — wearing her best maroon frock and her pearl
necklace and ear-rings. And someone like Carl Brisson to dance with, to flirt
with in the romantic moonlight.

She shivered and rubbed at her arms before drawing the curtains together;
shutting out the drab terraced-houses; blacking out her dreams.

"I'll put some more coal on," Jack noticed the shiver, "the nights'll soon be
getting lighter. Get January over and spring's just around the corner." Vera
shivered again and moved her chair closer to the fire.

"I feel chilled to the bone, Jack. I can't stop shivering."

"You've about caught a chill. It was like an igloo in the bedroom last night
wasn't it! Have we got any fever-powders in the cupboard? I should take one if
I were you."

When the children had been tucked up in bed Vera sat close to the fire and
worked on a cardigan she was knitting for Alexander.

Jack fiddled with the wireless, found some dance-music then had another
perusal of the Evening Post and smoked a cigarette.

"Jack....I'm feeling ever so funny!" Vera tried to keep her voice calm. "I feel
as though I'm on fire and yet I can't stop shivering."

Jack put his hand on her forehead.

"Yes, you're boiling hot. That powder must be working. It's getting rid of
your fever. I tell you what....make yourself a cup of cocoa and I'll put the
oven-shelf in the bed for you....get it nice and warm then you can go and get
into bed."

Jack lifted the oven-shelf out of the oven with a piece of old sheet. He
wrapped the sheeting round and round the shelf then took it upstairs and
placed it in Vera's side of the bed.

"Don't fancy cocoa tonight, Jack. It's a bit sickly. I think I'll make myself a
cup of Beefex and take it up to bed with me."

Vera put down the knitting and walked through to the scullery. She crumbled the Beefex cube into a cup and added boiling water. She took her nightdress from the airing cupboard at the side of the fire place and got undressed in front of the fire. She walked slowly up the stairs holding the cup of Beefex in front of her and sank gratefully into the warm bed.

Dong....dong....dong....Vera heard the chimes of Big-Ben heralding the nine o'clock news on the wireless. Jack had left the door at the bottom of the stairs slightly open and she could hear the wireless quite plainly.

A searing pain scythed across her stomach, she gasped and held on tightly to the top bedsheet. Another slash from the scythe....then another and another....up and up the pain spiralled bursting like a thousand exploding nails in her stomach, chest, throat and head.

She propped herself up with the pillows and looked out of the window. The curtains were not drawn together so she could see into the street below. A gas-lamp flickered low then spurted bright again, now low again almost going out altogether.

Vera pulled the clothes back and sat on the edge of the bed. She imagined that she could feel moisture between the tops of her legs but dare not take a look. Another pain, fiercer than the last attacked her body, she almost fainted from the shock waves it produced. She fumbled underneath the bed and pulled out the chamber pot then she crouched over it and clung onto the bedclothes for support.

Another onslaught of pain....then another....and another.

"Jack....! Jack....! Oh Jack....!"

Jack hurried up the stairs and stared in horror as he entered the bedroom and saw Vera crouching in the semi-darkness.

"I'm sorry, Jack....I'm sorry....but I did something this afternoon. I know I said I wouldn't do anything, I know I promised to leave things as they were, but I thought it would be for the best." She buried her face in the bedclothes and moaned in agony. "I can't stand it, Jack! I'm sorry, I'm trying not to make a noise so's the lads won't hear me, but I'm in agony....I think I'm going to die....I feel as though I'm going to die. God's punishing me, for killing my baby. I didn't mean to do it....I changed my mind."

Jack hurried over to the curtains and drew them together then he switched on the bedside-lamp. He stroked Vera's head and shoulders and said, "There, there," because he did not know what else to say.

"Fetch the doctor, Jack. Please go and fetch the doctor. Oh...... help me, Jack....help me....! I'm going to die, I know I'm going to die."

Jack rushed up Independent street and on to Alfreton road to where the doctor lived as though chased by demons from hell.

The doctor was due back now, said his wife smiling kindly at Jack, would Jack like to wait for a few minutes. Only a few minutes then he could tell the doctor what the trouble was. Jack told her he would leave a message — must get back to his wife.

At the very moment Jack left the doctor's house the foetus left Vera's body. Blood splattered down; adding more colour to the roses at the bottom of the pot; giving them a darker hue. Vera's life's blood intermingled with the afterbirth. Vera sat on the floor and stared into the pot. A tiny figure....no not a figure, an unreal thing and only just over an inch long. But she could see what it was — could make out the shape. She was certain she could make out the shape of arms and legs; was sure it had a face.

"I'm sorry, darling!....I'm so very sorry....!" she cried out and slumped to the floor, the racking sobs hurting her body even more than the earlier pains of abortion had done.

★ ★ ★ ★ ★ ★

"Come along now, young lady," the doctor helped Jack to lift Vera back on to the bed, "let's see what the trouble is shall we!"

An opening of black-bag, a listening through stethoscope and a shaking of medicine bottle. The doctor peered into the chamber-pot.

"Ah yes....yes....well there'll be quite a lot more blood to come, my dear, so don't be frightened. Now, I want you to mix this sedative for her," he turned to Jack, "and let's get some hot-water boiling shall we! Will you see to that for me?" He took off his jacket and rolled back his shirt-sleeves. "Nothing to be frightened of, my dear. You're going to be quite all right, but we must make sure that everything comes away." He felt her forehead and placed a thermometer underneath her tongue. "How many weeks gone were you — about twelve was it?" He removed the thermometer, peered at it and frowned ever so slightly.

"About eleven weeks, Doctor," Vera's voice was reduced to a whisper, "about eleven weeks I think."

"I see, I see," the doctor rummaged in the black-bag. "And would you like to tell me exactly what happened....umm?" His voice sounded normal and kind as though he were asking a child what she had been doing at school that day.

Vera turned her head to one side and stared towards the curtains then she closed her eyes tightly. Tears forced their way out of the sides of her eyes and cascaded down her cheeks gently splashing onto the bedclothes.

"All right, my dear. Now don't upset yourself." The doctor held both of her hands in his and gently squeezed them. "Don't upset yourself anymore, you're going to be all right. But in future, I want you to promise me that you won't be such a silly girl again."

Vera opened her eyes and looked at the doctor. His face was etched with kindliness; compassion; knowledge; reliability. Vera whispered what she had done to the baby and the burden shared lifted the ton weight from her heart but, unfortunately, not from her mind.

Jack returned to the room and the doctor whispered instructions. He must keep a good watch on her and if there was any change fetch the doctor at once. There may be complications but he hoped not, but if there was, Vera would have to be admitted to hospital and very quickly. But, at the present time, the doctor did not feel there was an emergency. He was hopeful that things would be all right.

After the doctor had left the house Jack switched off the bedside-lamp and left Vera alone for a while. Miraculously, the boys had not been disturbed by Vera's cries or, if they had woken at anytime, they had soon gone off to sleep again.

The light from the gas-lamp across the street suddenly came up bright again then, after a few seconds, spluttered and went out altogether.

Vera placed her hands on her stomach and thought, as she drifted into a drugged sleep, that it had been just like snuffing out a gas-light when she had killed her baby. One moment it had been safe and breathing quietly in the brightness and safety of her womb; then the next moment it had been engulfed in eternal darkness.

Vera went into the arms of Morpheus — her soul shrouded in grief. The doctor had rightly predicted that Vera would be all right but for the next few days she had to remain in bed. Maisie bustled about looking after the boys and doing the shopping and cooking and in a couple of weeks everything seemed back to normal.

Also, the terrible experience seemed to draw Vera and Jack closer together and they basked in the new rapport, grateful that Vera had not died, they were extra polite to one another, more attentive.

Like the January weather, their lives were rather drab, but now-and-again a few rays of sunshine and warmth burst through the gloom.

★ ★ ★ ★ ★ ★ ★ ★ ★ ★ ★ ★

CHAPTER EIGHT

January....February....March....April....the little Radford girls skipped away the days with their skipping-ropes and sang away the months with their childrens' games.

Everything was much the same in Nottingham. Men still queued, with shoulders hunched and eyes dull as they stood in line for dole-money and jobs. They talked of better things to come under the next government. The next government was bound to be better than this one. Got a lot to be thankful for, they said, things were much worse in Europe. Always plenty of trouble with those bloody hotheads abroad — as though there hadn't been enough killing in the Great War. But things would get better after the next election. Get a government with a bit of commonsense and there would be an end to job shortages; all the terrible poverty. That's what all the men in the Great War had died for. A better world to live in they had said, for their children.

Jack still dreamed of escaping from the factory. He sat at his cigarette machine and plotted an exciting future for himself.

Vera took life one day at a time and tried to erase the memory of the abortion from her mind.

In August, Maisie received a half-a-crown rise from the Carters, but she still helped herself to a few 'extras' and kept a piece of chalk in her handbag 'just-in-case'.

September proved to be as fruitful as its harvest for Alf who managed to get a job as night-watchman at the cycle factory and as he was also pulling in a few caddying jobs in the afternoons on Wollaton Park, his and Maisie's lifestyle had improved considerably.

In the evenings, when she was not working at the Carter's house, there was a bottle of stout for Maisie which she sipped whilst sitting on the chair near the door, looking out towards the railway station and the allotments which blossomed like miniature gardens-of-Eden amongst the drabness of Sodom. Apple-trees, pear-trees, plum-trees and damson-trees, branches spreading out as though protecting the rows of cabbages, peas and potatoes, and 'nobby-greens' — looking slightly incongruous nestling at the side of the grimy railway station with its coal-laden trucks and smoke-spouting trains, the engines smelling like a witch's brew of gas and sulphur.

Maisie sighed contentedly and wiggled her toes about in the new slippers with pom-poms on that Alf had bought for her last birthday. She stirred sugar into her cup of coffee and dipped a custard cream through the bubbles swirling round on the top of the drink.

Thursday was a nice day — a nothing much to do day. Bit of shopping from the corner shop, quick flip round the furniture with a duster and a bit of ironing to finish off.

Alf snored and twitched upstairs lost in his dream fantasies and it would be late afternoon before he poked his half-asleep, tousled head round the door and said, 'have you mashed then.'

After she had finished her coffee and biscuits Maisie put two irons on top of the gas-stove and lit the jets underneath them.

One or two shirts to iron, four cotton sheets to finish off and a pair of Alf's overalls to be given the once-over.

She cleared the table of pots and spread an old sheet, which she had folded into four, on top of the maroon chenille cloth. Now for a testing of iron by spitting on the surface. Maisie spat on one of the irons, the dancing, bubbling spit hissed up at her. Up-and-down....up-and-down....strong arms getting into a steady rhythm. The crumpled shirts straightening under the pressure, starch giving them a sparkling sheen like sunlight on water. Maisie loved the smell of freshly washed and starched clothes and often thought that that was what it must be like in heaven: everybody in clean, lightly starched nightgowns, smelling of fresh air and soap-powder.

A light tapping on the door. A voice calling, familiar, "It's me, duck." It was Nellie, a bundle in her arms which she cradled like a baby.

"Morning Maisie. Getting stuck into the ironing, are you?".

She took up her position on the chair near the door and sighed an extra large sigh.

"Just fetched mì best counterpane back from the pawnshop. Mrs. Johnson's back's playing her up again, so she asked me to do all her washing and ironing. You've never seen so many blouses, Maisie. But I needed a few extra bob so I'm not complaining. But they don't half take some ironing, some of her blouses."

"Is she still going out with that manager from the brewery?" Swish, swish, Maisie glided the iron over the shirt flap. "It's him that buys her all those lovely clothes. But she won't marry him, you know. I've heard he's asked her. Not once, but half-a-dozen times, but she's not having any."

"She told me she'd never remarry." Nellie put the bundle on the floor and unfastened the top two buttons of her coat. "After her Bertie got killed in the Great War she said she couldn't go through that agony again. And she's got a good job in Players offices. No, she said she'd never marry again."

"But he was killed nearly fifteen years ago!" Maisie walked through to the kitchen and spat on the other iron. "Ooh, I can't spit a tanner. Just let me finish this bit of ironing, Nell, and I'll mash a cup of tea."

"Her Bertie was one of the nicest blokes that breathed." Nellie looked sad. "It's like a beautiful love-story her life is. Fancy loving one man till the day you die! After he's been dead for years and years! I still love my old man but I wouldn't mind getting married again."

"I still love my Joseph," Maisie pressed down hard on the leg of an overall. "Doesn't mean because I married Alf that I don't still love Joe."

"I know that, Maisie," Nellie said hurriedly, "but I was just saying how romantic it was her never....."

....."I reckon I know why she won't marry him," Maisie interrupted her. "For a start, he's a boozer. They all are at the brewery. Can't see how they could be anything else, all that free ale. And for another thing, it'd put a stop to all those nice things he buys her. Keep 'em guessing a bit, dangle 'em on the end of a string, and they'll do anything for you. Once they put a ring on your finger you've had it."

"Well, I wish somebody'd put a ring on my finger." Nellie unfastened the rest of her coat buttons and stretched her legs out in front of her. "Somebody with a lot of money so's I could have a bit of a rest. A nice, home-loving man, who'd take good care of me and the lads."

"Oh ah! Got anybody we know in mind have you?" Maisie folded the ironing-sheet smaller and stored it away in the cupboard. "Somebody like the Pekoe-tips man, you mean? A nice steady type?"

Nellie turned crimson and fidgeted with her skirt.

"Nobody said anything about Bill Davenport. He's a nice enough bloke but nobody said anything about...."

...."Go on with you, Nell. You must think I'm daft or half blind. You're like a young girl the minute he steps foot inside the house. And don't think I haven't noticed you have your curlers in all morning when it's his delivery day." She laughed good humouredly. "Look at you now — with your ironworks underneath your turban — all ready for this afternoon." More laughter as she filled the kettle. "You must think I'm daft, you must."

Maisie walked back into the living-room and looked into the mirror above the fireplace which reflected the comings-and-goings of people on the avenue.

"Ey up....speak of the Devil....he's coming down the avenue now. He'll see you in your curlers, Nell. But it won't matter, will it! Not if you don't fancy him, it won't!"

Nellie leapt from her chair and hurried through to the kitchen. Maisie roared with laughter and said, "My mistake, Nell. It isn't him, but it looked very much like him from a distance."

Nellie joined in the laughter as she returned to her seat.

"You just wait, Maisie. You just wait. I'll get my own back on you. Hurry up with that cup of tea, I'm suffering from shock, you bogger you. And just for that, you can read my tea-leaves for free."

"Ah....the Pekoe-tips tea-leaves you mean!" Maisie poured milk into a cream-jug. "You'll be getting some free samples if you go about it the right way."

"Ooh, the way your mind works." Nellie folded her arms across her breasts, "I've never heard 'owt so daft." Her eyes lost their haunted look, there was a replacement of warmth which romance kindles. "Hey....have you ever noticed what a lovely big chest Bill Davenport's got?"

"What do you mean, Nell?" Maisie kept her face straight. "You mean his tea-chest, I presume!"

Both women laughed again and the budgie, in a cage on top of the sideboard, ran up-and-down on his perch and joined in the merrymaking with a nice bit of squawking.

Ten minutes later, the mournful whistle from a passing train whisked the two friends back into reality. Nearly dinner-time, there were things to be done.

The eleven thirty train from Alfreton had just snaked by and Maisie had potatoes to peel and pastry to make. And there was some shopping for Nellie to do and a large stack of her own ironing to tackle.

"See you about four then, Nell." Maisie smiled at Nellie. "And don't forget to take them curlers out. Get yourself 'done-up' for Mr. Davenport."

Nellie blushed again as she closed the door behind her and hurried up the avenue clutching the redeemed counterpane.

★★★★★★★★★★★★

CHAPTER NINE

"I was reading in the Evening Post last night about all the fighting that's still going on abroad. They're going barmy again in Spain, threatening a general strike; and the Hindus and Moslems are killing one another, right left and centre. And if there isn't a war between the Russians and Japanese before Christmas, my name's not Jack."

Jack sat upright in his seat and spoke loudly, wanting everyone in the canteen to know his views. "They never learn, do they! The fourteen eighteen war taught them nothing, some of 'em."

He looked round the table — no support there, he thought. A bunch of daft girls and women who wouldn't know what he was on about if there was fighting right here in Nottingham, smack in the middle of Slab Square.

"Fascists and communists, they're all the same if you ask me. Fill the working man up with a lot of twaddle, promise the moon and what do you get at the end of it!" He paused for affect. "A lot of dead men....that's what you get."

He looked at Len the foreman; a weak man, a crawler to the bosses. Len wouldn't be able to fight his way out of a paper-bag if he had a bayonet sticking in his arse, he thought.

"What would you do about all the trouble in the world, Len? About all the fascists? What would you do about the fascists?"

Jack's brain needed stimulation. He was so bored, he had almost fallen asleep at his machine that morning and he had had a terrible dream the night before.

Someone had chained him to his machine and the factory had closed down. They had left him alone, surrounded by millions of cigarettes, the stench of tobacco choking air from his lungs. Everyone else had gone to fight Fascists and Moslems and Russians.

And there had been blood trickling down the side of a hopper. Blood from Jack's lungs because he had caught T.B.. His lungs were disintegrating — being coughed up all over the hopper. He had woken up screaming and wet through with sweat and Vera had comforted him, let him make love to her. But it had not helped. The fumbling under the mattress for the french-letter, that almost put him off as much as the revolting cottonwool soaked in vinegar. The stroking of Vera's legs and Vera closing her legs together, reminding him of cold railway-tracks changing position when a train was approaching, sending the train on a different destination.

Jack stroking Vera's breasts and the nipples responding with their hardness but Vera lying there, passive and quiet as though he were an intruder — like a man shouting coarsely across a silent church.

"I said I'd machine-gun the lot of 'em". Len the foreman lit a cigarette and sucked the smoke down and down into his stomach.

Jack returned from his nightmare and withdrew from Vera's fantasy body.

"So would I....mow 'em all down. One of our neighbour's lad's gone and joined up this week."

Jack looked at the smiling females seated round the table.

"Set off up Independent street with a bag slung over his shoulder and only the clothes he stood up in. That's what they want, some good English blokes sorting 'em out. Best fighters in the world you know, the English blokes are." He tapped his head with his forefinger. "Got it up here. You have to use your noddle if you want to beat 'em."

The women nodded their heads and smiled a bit more. Men getting dressed up in uniforms and risking their lives was exciting to women, thought Jack bitterly. They queued up to see it on the pictures every week some of them. He imagined what the women were thinking, the images they held in their stupid brains. Glamorous uniforms, shiny brass buttons, gleaming bayonets and huge chargers galloping towards mounted, flashing guns. Let the boys play their war-games, so long as the women could play their games. Get married, have babies, and fill their houses with useless nick-nacks and expensive furniture that took nearly a lifetime to pay for.

God......! Jack looked at the women....what are they made of! And look at the way they used their bodies! The fantastic bargaining power they had. The prettier the girl the more power she had over a man. Sometimes the stupidest girl had superiority over a man if he lusted after her body.

A bell ended the tea-break and Jack was bustled along in the human stream heading for the machines.

Iris was in front of him; he watched her neat behind, tiny buttocks wrapped in a white overall reminding him of two apples swaying on the end of a branch.

I'd like to take a bite out of them, he thought, and smiled all the way back to his machine.

The machine gathered momentum and the cigarettes went into their dance.

I wonder if I could make a living selling things from a barrow! Jack closed his mind to his surroundings and journeyed on another fantasy trip. What could he sell? What did people need? People needed a roof over their heads; food; clothes; ale and sex. That was what most people needed to keep them happy.

He ground his teeth up-and-down. What could he sell that would make him rich enough to travel, and look after Vera and the kids at the same time? He wouldn't want to take Vera and the kids, not if he was going to travel a lot.

He had to think of something that people who were content to stay in one house and one job would be willing to buy. A necessity. His mind stamped a long list on a canvas of fresh-air. Vegetables....fruit....pots and pans....

cleaning materials. He rubbed out the list with a slight nodding of head. Something different — it had to be something different.

Iris was offering him a toffee. He smiled at her and popped the mint imperial into his mouth and thought, the age-old ploy, passed on by every woman since Eve had tempted Adam with the apple. Crafty 'aporths women were. Give you presents, do anything for you until they had you hooked. Dangling gifts and smiles, breasts and legs, pulling you gently, gently towards their charms then snap....they closed their legs and you were caught by your manhood, good-and-proper. Then it was all headaches and morning-sickness and funny turns.

Sunshine percolated its way through the wire-meshing on the windows at the back of the room; descended like a cloak of gold on Iris. Her hair, which she wore tied back for safety, was set on fire with colour.

Red-gold hair with natural waves that rippled down over her shoulders when combed loose.

Jack imagined the waterfall of red-gold hair cascading over black satin sheets and felt a terrible emptiness inside. The image faded and all that was left was blackness and the sound of rushing water through his brain.

What if he did eventually make love to Iris! What then! Things always had to go on. He would want more and more of her. Of those beautiful breasts, long slim legs and neat little behind. And what would Iris want? He knew damn well what Iris would want. She would want him....full-stop. His thoughts, feelings — everything sucked out of him until she thought she had possessed him completely. Then would come the bargaining with that beautiful body — driving him crazy until he had talked himself into believing he no longer loved his wife, deserting her and his children.

Then, as soon as Iris was sure of him — snap — caught by his manhood. He smiled to himself, waste of time Iris trying any of her tricks, he was immune. It had been like this with Vera, a hundred years ago it seemed now. Poor old Vera, how she had changed in the last couple of years.

Jack glanced up from the machine, Iris smiled at him. Red-gold hair, green cat's eyes, she smiled with white, even teeth from a pink, generous mouth.

God give me strength, thought Jack, as he heard the river flowing inside his head once again. He felt the line go taut as Iris pulled on the rod of temptation and drew him gently towards her out of the safety of the rocks.

★★★★★★★★★★★★

CHAPTER TEN

"Don't a bit of sunshine cheer-you-up!" Maisie took a hat from a paper bag and placed it on top of her head. "I thought summer was never going to come. It'll be July before you bat-your-eyeballs. After all that rain and the terrible floods, we deserve a bit of nice weather. Do you know the river flooded Clifton Colliery?" She tipped the hat to one side and looked at herself in the mirror. "One of Nellie's cousins works there and he lost some shifts because of the floods."

"I read about that in the Evening Post." Vera plopped jam in some tarts she had made. "Do you know the miners get over ten shillings a shift now? They get over ten shillings for a seven-and-a-hour shift. And they get free coal."

"They deserve it as well, crawling about in the dark on their hands and knees all the while. What do you think to my new hat, Vera? Gloria Swanson wore one like this in a picture where she was after this married man. She wore it tilted to one side like this. Do you think it suits me? I like the spots on the veil, don't you! It makes me look mysterious. It's a good hat for funerals. I like to look smart at funerals. Navy's much more flattering than black. I look washed-out in black."

"Jack doesn't like me in a hat." Vera took a tray of jam-tarts from the oven and placed them near the open scullery window to cool off. "He's never liked me in a hat. Says they make me look too old. Mind you, just lately, I feel old....as old as Methusela."

"Huh," Maisie tilted the hat to the other side, "what do men know about it." She handed the hat to Vera. "Here, you have a go. Go on, see how you look in it. You want to buy yourself a new hat. Marks and Spencers have got some lovely summery ones. You could get one with flowers on, cheer yourself up a bit. You've got the face for a hat. Your dad's sister Ethel would never go out without one, and you look like her you know."

Vera put the hat on her head and grimaced.

"I told you they don't suit me. And especially navy. I look too pale in navy. Perhaps I will buy one with flowers on, I've still got a bit of money left that Jack gave me out of his 'bonus'. This one definitely makes me look too pale." She handed the hat to Maisie.

"You'd look pale in anything lately." Maisie put the hat back in its bag and sat down. "What's worrying you, Vera? Haven't got yourself in a lot of debt have you, duck? If you want to borrow anything me and Alf's...."

"No, it's nothing to do with money. Well, we're always short of money of course, everybody is, but it's not that. I....I haven't been sleeping very well lately and when I do get off to sleep I have nightmares and wake up wet through with perspiration. Sometimes my nightgown's wringing wet. All round my chest and back."

"You ought to go to the doctor's." Maisie's face was a field of ploughed, worried furrows.

"I did go to see him and he said it was quite normal, you know, a reaction from losing the....from losing the baby. He gave me some sleeping tablets but Jack doesn't like me taking them. He says you can get addicted to things like that and he's put me off taking them."

"Take half-of-one then and don't tell him." Maisie always full of advice and wisdom. "It's all right for him, he could sleep on a clothes-line, couldn't he. You get yourself better, n'mind about what he says."

Maisie let out a shriek. "Ooh, you little bogger. Wait till I get hold of you. Look Vera, look what he's done to my hat."

Alexander, unusually quiet behind the sofa, had decided to put Maisie's new hat on Rupert, the family's long-suffering cat. Rupert slept on, unperturbed and half-hidden by the veiled Gloria Swanson hat.

The two women laughed heartily and Maisie chased Alexander into the front-room. She caught hold of him and lifted him into the air, gave him a smacking kiss on the cheek, and walked back into the kitchen with him in her arms.

"You're a naughty monkey." She kissed him again. "That's grammar's best hat."

"He's getting to be a right handful." Vera emptied the tarts on to a cooling-tray then put more tarts into the oven. "I get worn out, three little 'uns to look after. I never get any time to myself. Except when you have them on a Monday of course. But I don't get much of a rest because there's all the washing to do."

"I tell you what," Maisie smiled an inspirational smile, "now the weather's cheering up a bit, I'll take them for a picnic. I'll take them to Trent Bridge this Sunday."

"You can't manage all three of them, mam."

"'Course I can. Alf and me'll have them for the whole day and that'll give you a nice break."

"Oh, they're too much of a handful, mam. 'Specially Alex. You have to watch him like a hawk."

"Think I can't handle my own grandchildren! I shall enjoy a nice picnic."

"All right then, if you're sure you can manage. I'll pack some food for you."

"No, I'll see to that. Some sandwiches, a few cakes and biscuits and a flask of tea, and a few bottles of pop. I hope it's a nice hot day. We'll catch a trolley to Trent Bridge then we'll walk down the Victoria Embankment to the toll-bridge down Wilford. There's some lovely picnic spots down there. That's where me and your dad did most of our courting, near the toll-bridge."

Maisie planned ahead and tried on her new hat again.

"I think it looked better on the cat," she remarked, then giggled like a school girl.

"I knew it would be a lovely day." Maisie put down her shopping basket which was laden with picnic food and drink. "There was a lovely red sky last night. I said to Alf, didn't I Alf, it'll be a scorcher tomorrow. Red sky at night....shepherd's delight."

"I wouldn't mind being a shepherd, would you, Jack!" Alf winked at Jack. "'Nowt to do all day but sit and watch the world go by and look at a bunch of daft sheep nibbling at grass. You could take your 'snap' and a couple of bottles of ale and live like the lord-of-the-manor."

"Bit nippy in the cold weather though, Alf." Jack put his Sunday Express to one side and lit a cigarette.

"Like a fag, Alf?"

"No thanks, sooner have me pipe." Alf fumbled in his pocket.

"Well don't get lighting it up yet." Maisie helped Dougie with his coat, "stinking our Vera's house out with that mucky thing."

"Can we go to the Pleasure Boats, grammar?" Frankie pulled at Maisie's coat. "Can we, grammar?"

"You wait and see, duck. We've got the whole day to do lots of things."

"Have you packed their cricket bat and stumps, Vera? We'll have a game of cricket. Grammar can field, 'cause she can't hit the ball, can she!" Alf drummed his thumb-nail on the stem of his pipe. "Can't hit the ball for toffee, can she!"

"Oh, hark at Test-Match Charlie then." Maisie put her hands on her hips and laughed good-humouredly. I'm a good bowler, aren't I, Frankie?"

"Yes, but you're not supposed to aim it at my head, Maisie. You're supposed to aim for the bat, isn't she Frankie?"

Alf winked at Dougie and Frankie who giggled and fidgeted about; anxious as keyed-up thoroughbred horses straining to be set free for their day out at Trent Bridge.

Vera fastened the straps on Alexander's reins.

"Better keep him in his reins, mam. He's like greased lightning. Keep him in his reins and watch him like a hawk, else he'll be off."

"Oh, stop whittling, Vera. Don't forget I've had kiddies of my own. Right....are we all ready then!"

She bustled the children out of the back-door and down the entry.

"See you about eight then."

The excited voices of the children floated into the shiny, summer morning and drifted away until a faint echo.

★ ★ ★ ★ ★ ★

Jack put his arm around Vera's waist and kissed her cheek.

"Just like we're courting again, love. Remember when we first moved in here? Lazy Sundays, all peaceful and quiet? It's just like we were courting again, being all on our own."

"Yes," she replied, and looked at him but did not see him. "Just like we're courting again."

She straightened her pinafore and gently edged away from him. Neither of us really believe that, she thought sadly, you can never, ever go back. Like the womb, the safety of the womb, you can never return. Thrills are the fore-runners of disillusion. Like a first party dress....first taste of whisky....first grown-up kiss....first entwining of lovers' bodies. You remember — but you can never recapture.

Vera tried to recall her feelings, that first time in the entry when Jack had kissed her, but she could not remember how she had felt, no matter how hard she tried.

A sadness swirled all around her like a mist of sighs and she felt as though she had lived forever.

★★★★★★

"Look grandad, there's some rowing-boats." Dougie tugged at Alf's jacket. "When can we go on the Pleasure Boat?"

"Perhaps we'll go on a boat this afternoon." Alf took hold of Dougie's hand, "We've got to have a game of cricket first."

"There's some swans over there. Look grammar, swans!" Frankie skipped on ahead. "Can we feed the swans?"

"When we've had our picnic. We'll save them some crusts." Maisie looked towards the swans and their majestic beauty brought a tight feeling to her throat. She had brought her own sons to feed the swans; and they had laughed and skipped and said the same things her grandsons were saying. Happy, lively, perfect little boys. Beautiful children throbbing with life — growing towards the screeching bombs and filthy, churned-up mud.

"Look how the sun's catching the water, Maisie." Alf shielded his eyes. "It's just like somebody's tipped gallons of gold paint all over the river."

He shifted the shopping basket from his left arm to the other.

"Going to be a right scorcher. We'll all get sunburnt. Your mam'll think she's got little black lads when she sees you."

"I've brought a bottle of olive-oil." Maisie looked at the river painted with gold. "I'll rub plenty of olive-oil on us. We'll be fried to a frazzle. And you'd better keep your sun-hats on, boys. Don't want you to get sunstroke 'else your mam won't let us take you out again."

"What's sunstroke, grammar?" Frankie was at the 'what's that' age.

"Your hair catches on fire," said Alf, who was at the 'acting daft' age.

Frankie pulled at his hat, made sure the sun could not get at his hair. Dougie did the same and kept close to Alf in case he needed grandad to put out his blazing hair.

But within a few minutes it was all forgotten. Dougie and Frankie again ran on ahead, exploring.

Next came Alf carrying the shopping basket and an old blanket for them to sit on. He puffed away contentedly on his stoked-up pipe.

Maisie lagging behind, holding on to Alexander's reins with one hand, and a handbag laden with clean nappy, sponge-bag, towel, flannel, olive-oil and numerous other things, in the other hand.

It was a golden day. Golden sun....golden river....golden laughter....golden sky. One of those days that money could not buy — it stretched out in front of them and all for free.

★★★★★★★★★★★★

CHAPTER ELEVEN

Maisie selected a place for the picnic on the other side of the Suspension Bridge — Alf put the basket down gratefully then spread the blanket on the grass for them to sit on.

"Good spot near these trees, Maisie."

"Ah, we'll be needing plenty of shade by the looks of that sun. Who wants a nice drink of pop then? I've got your favourite....cream soda."

The bottle released its screw-top with a hiss and the boys clambered round with their cups.

"Sit down....sit down now if you're having some pop," bossed Maisie, "it's dangerous to run about with a cup in your hand."

The boys plopped down on the grass, hands outstretched for the sparkling cream-soda water.

"I'll have a drop if there's any left, Maisie." Alf put his pipe back into his pocket. "That walk's give me a right thirst. I'm that weak I shan't be able to lift the cricket bat." He winked at the boys. "One of you lot had better bat first. Give grandad a chance to get his wind back."

"Are you all right, Alf? Chest not bothering you is it?"

"No....take more than a whiff of Jerry's gas to scupper a tough 'un like me. My lungs are like a pair of giant's bellows." He hammered on his chest like Tarzan did in the jungle pictures. "It's me legs that keep conking out just lately. They say 'as the legs are the first to give out." He laughed suggestively.

"I don't know about that," Maisie poured him a drink. "After what happened last Saturday night I thought summat else was beginning to give out."

They laughed easily together, enjoyed the secret joke. The children latched onto the happy mood and smiled and laughed with their grand-parents; the scene was set for a most enjoyable day.

Alf hit the ball with the edge of the bat, the ball rocketed skywards then zoomed in on Maisie who opened her arms and mouth, tried hard to catch it and missed.

"Ooh....grandma's got butterfingers. You don't have to catch it in your mouth, Maisie. That don't count you know."

"The sun was in me eyes. Can't see the ball when the sun's in me eyes." Maisie ran after the ball and threw it to Frankie who was bowling.

"Aim for the wicket, Frankie." Maisie cupped her hands to her mouth and shouted encouragement. "Give him one of your over-arms. Go on....give him a fast one. Aim at grandad's legs, Frankie."

"Ooh, you're a good 'un, you are. Don't forget I haven't got me box on." Alf tapped the grass in front of the wicket stumps. "Put a stop to your fun-and-games if the ball catches me unawares."

"Ooh," Maisie was girlish and silly, "what sort of box are you talking about then....a match-box!"

"You cheeky beggar." Alf grinned at her.

"Watch out, grandad." Dougie jumped up and down excitedly as Frankie aimed the ball.

The ball bounced and flew over Alf's head. Everyone shrieked with laughter.

"That was a close one, Frankie," Alf grinned at him, "I was nearly out there....head before wicket."

More laughter dancing on warm air, tossed by a gentle breeze across the rippling, sun-caressed water.

Frankie bowled again, Alf stepped craftily to one side and let the ball smack into the wicket.

"Ooh, you got me that time, Frankie. Come on, Dougie, you're in next."

"I want to bat. Me want a go." Alexander ran towards the stumps.

"In a minute, my love. You stand here near grandma and help me catch the ball." Maisie patted his head. "We'll have an ice-cream in a bit. Look out for the ice-cream cart and we'll all have a cornet."

Alexander forgot about batting and scanned the horizon for the ice-cream cart.

Alf and Maisie tried hard to keep the game of cricket exciting but within ten minutes all three boys had lost interest. Interiors of bushes had to be explored and accessible trees needed to be climbed. Other children had to be weighed up and cows had to be viewed from a safe distance.

Cricket stumps and bat lay abandoned on the grass, Alf and Maisie sank gratefully onto the blanket.

"Don't wander away," Maisie tired but ever watchful, "keep where we can see you."

Alf lit his pipe and leaned back against the trunk of a tree.

"Wouldn't it be nice if we could live near the river! Little bungalow at the side of the river would be just-the-job for you and me."

"What about the winter-time though?" Maisie toyed with Alexander's rein," be a bit miserable in the winter-time. It'd be ever so damp and cold. I don't think I'd fancy it. I'm not a swan....might be all right for the swans."

"Feed the swans, grammar," Alexander put his arms around Maisie's neck, "feed the swans."

"Soon, when we've had our picnic, duck. We'll save them some crusts. Make their feathers curly, crusts will. If you eat all your crusts up it makes you have curly hair you know. Now then, are you looking out for that ice-cream cart? Can you see the ice-cream man yet? You're going to have a nice cornet in a minute."

Maisie shielded her eyes with her hand and looked back towards the

Victoria Embankment. "There's a crowd over there look. They're all standing round the ice-cream cart. Get some pennies ready grandad, and we'll all have a cornet."

Alf sorted out some half-pennies. "Good job grandad's millionaire, 'int it Alex!"

"Yes, I only married you for your money."

"I thought it was my blue eyes you fell for?"

"It was....but it was your money that swayed me."

"Wonder what they're doing over there, Maisie? All that machinery and stuff? There's dredgers and all sorts." Alf pointed with the stem of his pipe. "And look at all those heaps of sand and earth." He nodded at Alexander. "Big sand-castles aren't they, Alex. I'll take you to have a look in a bit. You 'ought to have brought your bucket and spade."

"Now don't you get him mucked-up. He's got his best shoes on. I'll bet they're going to build some sort of dam because of the floods. Time they did something 'an all. People's cellars swimming in filthy water. It was really bad this year wasn't it! I'm glad we don't live down The Meadows."

"Saves 'em going all the way to Venice for a holiday. They just have to sit back and wait for the floods and 'Bobs-your-uncle'".

"Aah....only instead of going down the street on a gondola, you go on a sofa or an armchair." Maisie shuddered. "Oh dear, it must take weeks for everything to dry out. You wouldn't catch me living down The Meadows for all the tea in china."

The ice-cream man peddled towards them and in a few minutes lips and tongues were licking and sucking on delicious creamy cornets from the Italian man's cart.

Alf took out a large white handkerchief and wiped his mouth, then he tied a knot in each corner of the handkerchief and put it on his head and pulled comical faces at the boys.

"Cost you seven-and-six at Dunn's hat-shop this would." He tapped his head.

"Ooh, what do you look like!" Maisie laughed at him, "you look half simple."

"Well, I forgot to bring me panama hat. When I wear my panama I look like Clark Gable when he was in that picture with Norma Shearer. What was it called now....! oh yes, it was 'A Free Soul'".

"That handkerchief makes you look like a simple soul." Maisie undid the top two buttons of her dress and leaned back against an oak tree. "We'll take our shoes and socks off in a bit and have a paddle. We'll just dabble our feet in the water, it'll cool us off a bit. And this afternoon, we'll all go on the Pleasure-Boat up to Colwick. But you've got to be good lads."

"Look what I've got here." Alf fished about in the picnic things and held up two comics and a picture-book. "You come and have a look at this picture-book with grandad." He held out his arms to Alexander and gave Dougie and Frankie a comic each.

Maisie closed her eyes and drifted into a gentle snooze; her mouth relaxed, smiling at someone in her dream.

Alf looked at Maisie and could picture the lovely girl she had once been. The young woman her husband and boys had known before obscene death had carved despair on her hopes and youth. Alf had seen a photograph of her, but it was not the same, he thought.

He turned another page for Alexander and thought, I'm a damned lucky bloke. Take some beating what I've got, it would. Cracking little night-watchman's job and a few bob for caddying. Smashing missis, with a good sense-of-humour and a nice cuddly figure. And we've got a decent roof over our heads. Chest plays me up a bit sometimes on account of Jerry's gas, but it could have been a lot worse. Could have had my legs blown off or my brains blown out.

He turned another page and looked at Maisie again. Blowed if I don't buy her a nice bunch of flowers tomorrow, he thought. A blinking great big bunch.

"There's a pussycat." Alf pointed to the cat grinning on page three of the picture-book.

"Grammar's hat," Alexander patted the page.

"No....pussycat." Alf persisted gently.

"Grammar's hat," repeated Alexander loudly. "Rupert."

"Ah well, you could be right I suppose, me lad." Alf gave in. "Some of grandma's hats do look like dead cats."

★ ★ ★ ★ ★ ★

At halfpast-twelve Maisie handed out cheese and tomato sandwiches, and potted meat sandwiches — cut at a funny angle, all dainty like she did for the Carters, the portions triangular shaped instead of square. After the sandwiches came home-made sponge-cake oozing with raspberry jam and a chocolate-roll that had got a bit squashed and was flat instead of round.

The boys clambered for more pop; Maisie and Alf enjoyed tea from a flask; a few birds joined in the picnic, fluttering nervously in and out of the crusts that Maisie had thrown to them, then twittering in triumph as they clamped their beaks on a piece of bread.

"I've saved something for the swans," Maisie drained the last drop from her teacup and looked at the tea-leaves in the bottom. "There's water in my teacup," she tilted the cup to one side.

"There's tea in mine," Alf mimicked her, "did you forget to put any tea in yours then?" The two older boys giggled. "Perhaps Nellie Tealeaf's hiding somewhere. She's about ate 'em while you weren't looking, Maisie."

"You daft thing. I'm reading my leaves. I can see a river ever so plain."

"If you look over there, you'll see a river ever so plain won't she, lads! Wouldn't get it in a teacup though."

More giggling from Frankie and Dougie.

"I'll have a piece of that chocolate-roll please, Maisie. Then when I've finished you can read the crumbs on my plate. If I leave any that is. I might lick me plate if nobody's looking."

"Don't teach the boys bad manners, Alf. You know they copy everything you do and say. It's rude to lick plates isn't it, boys?"

"Dad licks his plate when he's had pudding and custard." Dougie grinned.

"Anybody want a drop more pop?" Maisie changed the subject and put her teacup down. "Look out for some swans, 'cause we've got some crusts left for them. They love a nice bit of brown bread."

"I'll have that last piece of chocolate-roll if you don't want it, Maisie." Alf licked chocolate from his fingers. "Don't want the swans fighting over it." He looked at the boys. "Them swans fight like billy-oh over your grandma's chocolate-roll you know. I had to fetch a policeman to 'em last time, to help me to separate them. There was about fifty swans there was....all scrapping over grandma's chocolate-roll."

"Ooh, I don't know how you think 'em up!" Maisie wiped the boys' hands with a damp flannel. "You're a bigger liar than Tom Pepper you are, Alf."

"Now then Maisie....own up to it. You're the best cook in Radford. Them swans swim all the way from Colwick once they get a whiff of your baking. I'll bet they've smelt it already."

The boys all turned towards Colwick, eyes searching the river for the fifty hungry swans.

Another family spread a tablecloth nearby, the parents nodded and smiled at Maisie and Alf. A boy, about the same age as Frankie, kicked a football halfheartedly and smiled encouragingly at the two older boys, whilst his young sister fussed with a rag-doll.

The three boys were soon running noisily after the football. The grown-ups rested in the shade of the elm trees and Alexander, who had been fighting against falling asleep, curled into a ball and gave in with a sigh.

"Don't go near that machinery," Alf pointed towards the dredgers parked at the edge of a sand-bank, "keep away from those piles of rubble, there's good lads."

He lit his pipe once again and stared contentedly across the river and thought that he really must talk Maisie into having a riverside bungalow when they were old.

Maisie drifted off to sleep again, lying on her back with Alexander's rein wound round her left wrist.

Happy sounds everywhere. Chirruping sparrows; lazy moo from a cow in the next field; excited bark from a young mongrel dog who was also chasing the football; laughter from the three boys as they jostled each other: all the sounds blending as though part of a beautiful concerto.

"GRAMARR.........! GRAMARR........!"

An ice-cold vice grabbed at Maisie's heart and she thought the beat would never start up again. Terror in the voice that called out to her held her mind completely senseless for five seconds.

She sat up — Alf was running towards the machinery — the piles of sand and earth. He was snatching at the laces of his shoes. Alf flung himself into the air, arms stretched out awkwardly, then he disappeared down the side of the sand-bank.

More men ran to the water's edge; their actions seemed to Maisie as though everything had been speeded-up. Like a Goose Fair roundabout gone haywire....everything going round and round, the noise getting louder. The noise was getting deafening. People running from every direction the men shouting, the women screaming. The women screamed as though their voice boxes had gone out of control, it seemed to Maisie as though they would scream forever.

She told herself it was a nightmare. "Wake up!" she cried out, her words mingling in the air with the screams. "Wake up!"

She looked round for Frankie and Dougie and the other little boy — but she knew it was them — could tell by the way she felt. The same horror enveloped her that had been there when they had told her about her own boys.

"Dear God....oh dear God....take me now....fill me with cancer....blind me....anything God....but please let my babies be safe."

She thought that God had struck a bargain with her and made her paralysed, because when she tried to stand up she could not control her legs. She knelt on the blanket then slumped forward and stayed in a crouching position, still holding on to Alexander's rein.

A large crowd gathered near the water's edge. Now they divided into two groups and Maisie saw that they were making way for Alf.

Alf held one of the boys in his arms, she could not tell which one, another man followed behind him, also holding a child.

"Two," Maisie mumbled to herself, "two....two."

The policeman was young — too young to be able to hide the great distress he was feeling. He spoke softly to Alf, and stared at the grass, as though ashamed of the questioning.

"And er....the bank just gave way, sir? The boys were running after the football and the bank just collapsed underneath them?"

Alf nodded a reply.

"And er....you dived in straight away, but you couldn't see anything at first because the water was very muddy?"

Alf also stared at the grass.

"It was just like somebody had tipped gold-paint all over the water. You ask my missis, she'll tell you." Alf did not seem to comprehend. "Nobody'd believe how muddy it was underneath. I couldn't see 'owt."

"Then you dived down a second time, saw one of the boys and grabbed for him? That was the little chap there, sir. Timothy Whiteman?"

"He was paddling like a dog, right near the bottom. Paddling just like a dog and I grabbed at his hair."

"I see, sir. Well, that young chap's going to be all right. Frightened him a bit of course, but he'll be all right." The policeman wrote something in his note-book. "And you say you dived in again....got hold of one of the other boys?", the policeman chewed the end of his pencil and talked more softly, "but by the time you had got him out of the water, there was no sign of life?"

"You wouldn't have believed how muddy it was underneath....not after seeing how clear it was on top." The tears rolled down Alf's cheeks and mingled with the river water that was trickling down from his hair.

"I just couldn't see 'owt for the mud and that....not once the bank had collapsed in the river you see."

"Yes, I see. And Mr. Whiteman dived in to help you and....and he recovered the body of your other grandson....er....Douglas....?"

A horrified gasp came from the crowd. They passed the information, to those who had not heard, in sympathetic whispers. Two grandsons, he had said. Two grandsons — both drowned in front of their grandparents' eyes!

One little lad, their pal, had been saved, and the mongrel dog had scrambled out further down the river. But the two brothers had fallen in the muddiest part and the men had not been able to find them right away. The two brothers had drowned together, on this beautiful, sunny summer's day.

The crowd seemed mesmerised by the double tragedy and could not move away. They ought to do something to help, they told one another, needed to do something to help....but what....? Two children were dead....there was nothing they could do....nothing at all.

A bell-clanging ambulance approached and kindly ambulance-men, assisted by a police-sergeant, took control.

Timothy, Alf and Mr. Whiteman were to go to the General Hospital and be treated for shock. Maisie also had to see a doctor.

It was agreed that the police-sergeant and young constable would go and break the awful news to Vera and Jack and they also offered to take charge of Alexander. The crowd drifted away, eyes averted from Maisie and Alf.

Just before the ambulance-door slammed shut, Alf caught sight of the glistening, golden river.

"Everything looks just the same," he clasped the red hospital blanket to himself and tried to breathe properly. "Just the same, Maisie."

"Nothing will ever be the same." Maisie fiddled with the top on the empty cream-soda water bottle lying in her basket; and with one last great effort, renounced God with all her being.

★★★★★★★★★★★★

CHAPTER TWELVE

Vera awakened but dare not open her eyes. The horror of the day which awaited her clasped her body in numbness, making her feel as though she would never be able to walk again.

She listened to Jack's steady breathing and envied him the oblivion. Her boys were downstairs....in eternal oblivion.

She told herself they were only sleeping and that any time now she would hear laughter and boy-noisy, happy voices.

If I could die, just cease to breathe, then everything would be all right, she thought. But I shall have to continue, maybe live to be very old, so that I can go on-and-on being punished for what I did to my baby.

Her mind travelled back again to that cold afternoon; the clock ticking at the bedside; quietness and the feeling of being terribly afraid. Once more the Slippery-Elm Bark destroyed her baby and part of her mind. She curled herself into a ball and moaned inside, clenching her teeth together so that no sound could escape. Her boys were downstairs....and she was being punished.

Vera opened her eyes and looked at the clock — it was only twenty-two-minutes to seven. Nearly another hour before the alarm went off.

There were footsteps outside. Workmen's footsteps — the rhythmic clinking of the metal-blakeys men used, to save the cost of paying for new heels on their boots.

They could tap-dance in those boots, Vera thought, and tried to concentrate on the men tap-dancing to work.

Her boys were downstairs....and would never go to work.

Milk-bottles clinked together and the heels of the workmen were now joined by the steady clip-clop of horses hooves. The milkman was making his way down Independent street with his horse-and-cart.

A dog barked from a backyard somewhere. It was a half-hearted bark, as though the dog was still sleepy and could not be bothered to put his whole heart into it; but dogs were expected to warn people when milkmen, breadmen and postmen arrived so he had to earn his saucer of cold tea and a few scraps.

Vera's mind searched frantically for every single memory of that last morning. That sunny Sunday morning when the boys had skipped off down the entry, eager to get to the water.

She tried to remember every word that had been said. Had she kissed them goodbye — given them a hug — treated them lovingly? But everything was all mixed up. Yes....she had kissed them. She began to sweat again. No, wait....they had kissed her. Perhaps they'd thought she didn't want to kiss them! She panicked and tortured herself further. Maybe she had been a little off-hand with them!

But they had been eager to go on the picnic! And surely they knew how much she loved them! But I didn't tell them! A feeling of nausea began in her stomach and edged upwards towards her throat. I never told them how much I loved them, she agonised, because I thought they could tell. I never smacked them too hard, and I always tried to give them the meals they liked best.

I'm a good mother....I am....I am. They knew I loved them, I know they did. They must have done, mustn't they!

This time she could not control the moan, it was the first thing that Jack heard that day.

He opened his eyes and as realisation forced itself upon him he clung to Vera as though he too were drowning. Vera sobbed on his shoulder — the day had begun.

Jack filled the kettle and lit the gas-stove. He switched on the lights in the scullery and kitchen because the curtains would remain closed until after the funeral.

He went over to the mantlepiece and fumbled for his cigarettes. He looked round the room at the orderliness and the coldness. Vera had tidied and polished the furniture the night before, not a trace remained of Frankie and Dougie's existence.

Pieces of black cloth were draped over all the pictures hanging on the walls. Black....black....black.

That's what life is, Jack thought hopelessly, it's all blackness. He looked across to the front-room door and wanted to go and have a look at his boys but could not do so. He felt afraid of them and was deeply ashamed.

The kettle began to boil, Jack stared at the steam. He wanted to hate somebody for causing the terrible tragedy. It was Maisie's fault, Alf's fault, the council's fault.

No-one's fault, said a voice inside his head. He picked up the kettle and with trembling hands poured water on to the tea-leaves.

★ ★ ★ ★ ★ ★

Maisie, Alf and Nellie arrived at the house just after half-past-nine. They had arranged for Nellie to get the food ready for the mourners, when they returned to the house. She, and Mrs. Dexter the 'laying-out' woman who lived on Edinburgh Street, would stay behind and see to everything. Alex too would be in their care because Vera did not want him to go to the cemetery.

The hearse was to arrive at the house at ten-thirty and would carry the coffins up to the General Cemetery at the top of Alfreton Road.

There were a few distant relatives and some had come from as far away as Ripley and Mansfield. Cousins, Alf's half-brother and his family, and an old aunt of Maisie's and a step-uncle. Relations who only met for deaths and marriages had all turned up to show their last respects; and to take part in the mourning; and try to help the grieving parents through the day.

Everyone was dressed in black. What they did not have or could not afford they borrowed from friends and neighbours. Highly polished black shoes and boots, housed black-stockinged feet. Black scarves, ties, armbands for the men. Black silk-blouses, hats and veils, and dresses for the women.

One-by-one they filed in silence in to the tiny house and one-by-one they went to look at the boys lying in their silk-lined coffins.

One-by-one they touched the boys so that the memory of such a sight would not haunt their dreams — a superstition passed on from generation to generation, its origin no-one knowing nor questioning.

The sun tried in vain to find a way through a chink in the curtains. It was a nice day outside....warm enough for a picnic.

Alf answered a knock at the back door. A tearful woman thrust a wreath into his hands and hurried away after saying, "There's a card".

Alf read the words on the card out aloud to the family.

'To Frankie and Dougie from all the children on Independent Street. Suffer Little Children To Come Unto Me'.

Alf put the card and wreath on the table and cried unashamedly. Maisie put her arms around him and for some strange reason thought about how she and Vera had laughed about funeral hats. Like to look smart for a funeral, she had joked, and laughed about it. Now, it did not matter whether she looked smart or not — and the hat was black not navy. A small, black felt hat with a heavy black veil.

Why do we say such awful things, she thought, as she held on to Alf's shoulder then stroked it like she would a dog or cat.

★★★★★★

The funeral director stepped inside the front-room, black top-hat held respectfully underneath his left arm. Four bearers followed him into the house and stood silently awaiting their instructions.

"Would the Mother like to see her children for the last time before er....before we....", the kind undertaker spoke quietly, solemnly.

"Yes," Jack answered him even more quietly, "I'll go and fetch her." He went into the kitchen and bent over Vera. "Vera....they're here, love. Come and say goodbye to the boys." He helped her from the chair and ushered her gently into the front-room.

Hand-in-hand they looked for the last time into the tiny silk-lined coffins. At their children sleeping peacefully; dressed in white gowns embroidered with forget-me-nots; white marble faces and white marble hands resting on white marble chests.

People everywhere....everywhere. They had come from all over Radford to watch. The crowds filled the pavements, spilled on to the road, stood on doorsteps, looked through bedroom windows. In Radford, everyone wanted to be part of a funeral. Women with babies in their arms, men on the dole, men on night-shifts who stayed up until it was over. Shopkeepers and tradesmen, hats and caps pressed against chests, old and young they lined the streets to pay their last respects to the two little boys.

Jack, Vera, Maisie, and an old aunt who was crippled with arthritis, climbed up into the seats at the back of the hearse.

The driver pulled gently on the reins, released the brake, and the two jet-black, blinkered horses tossed their heads in readiness. Now they started to walk and the cortege began the slow journey to the General Cemetery.

The undertaker walked slowly in front, setting the pace. The four bearers walked two on either side of the hearse and Alf, the other relatives and the rest of the mourners, walked behind.

On any other day a crowd as large as the one which lined Independent Street would have made a tremendous noise but, on that morning, there were only three predominant sounds.

The steady clip-clop of the 'bury-horses'; a cry from a baby; and the agonised voice of Alf as he said over and over again to the hushed onlookers, "It was muddy, you see....I couldn't see 'owt."

★ ★ ★ ★ ★ ★ ★ ★ ★ ★ ★ ★

CHAPTER THIRTEEN

"Are you going down Goose Fair, Jack?" Iris tucked a strand of hair behind her left ear and smiled at Jack.

"Might go down Saturday afternoon, take the lad for an hour. Are you going down?" Jack answered her.

"Want him to take you on the 'Cocks', do you?" Bette joined in their conversation. "Everybody likes a ride on the cocks, 'specially on the Forest when it's dark."

"Shut up, Bette, you are awful," Iris blushed, glanced shyly at Jack, then concentrated on the cigarettes.

"You might get him to buy you a cock-on-a-stick if you're nice to him," Bette laughed raucously, enjoying Iris' embarrassment.

"I used to do some of my courting on the Forest you know," Bette continued, "up against the roller."

"I've heard about that roller," Jack encouraged her, "they ought to have a plaque put on it I reckon, don't you! It'll go down in history as the most famous grass-roller in England."

"What are you two talking about?", Iris smiled at Jack, "what roller, where?"

"On the Forest in front of the pavillion," Bette butted in again, "a great big grass-roller that they do the cricket-pitch with. Let your boyfriend bend you backwards over that and you'll know about it, won't she, Jack!"

"Shut up, Bette, you get worse. Iris wouldn't know about things like that. She's a young, innocent girl."

"Huh....these young 'uns know more than we do nowdays," Bette fed the machine more cigarettes. "The old man's taking me down the Fair on Friday night. He likes to go and gawp in the Wall-of-Death. Watch all them barmy boggers going up the sides of the walls on their motor-bikes. And he likes the dart-stalls as well. He nearly always wins something on the darts. It's a load of rubbish but he's like a big daft kid when he wins a cheap butter-dish or a glass ashtray."

"I like the steam-boats," Iris enthused, "and going round the sideshows. They had a lovely Sleeping-Beauty last year — and the smallest man in the world was there."

"Can't be," Bette waited for a few seconds to get their full attention. "My old man's got the smallest in the world." Her laughter reverberated all around the room.

Jack laughed with her and was grateful. The past few months had held little enough laughter for him. It was there all the time — that awful melancholy. And, even if he did forget for a little while during the daytime, the terrible depression was still there every waking morning and each night before he went to sleep.

The worst horror was when he could not remember what Frankie and Douglas had looked like. Sometimes, he could imagine their faces, but there was dreadful moments when he could not picture their features at all. These were the times he looked at the photographs wrapped in tissue-paper inside his wallet. The two smiling faces assured him that yes....they really had existed. Held out their arms to him; climbed onto his lap; come running for bandages for bloody knees; hugged and kissed him before they went to sleep at night.

The vaguer their images the more he needed to remember them. Dozens of times a day the horror of their deaths surged through him, making him dizzy and weak. At times like these he was grateful for any kind of diversion, even welcomed Bette's inane conversation, her crude jokes.

Anything's better than remembering about the boys' deaths every single minute of the day, he thought, and decided to buy Bette some chocolates for Christmas.

Bette had been the most help to him, just after the boys had drowned. She had collected for a wreath and there had been lots of money left over which she insisted be used to buy something for Alexander.

Bette had made him talk about the tragedy, where others had avoided him, changed the subject and averted their eyes when he walked by them. But Bette had put her arm around him and held on tightly to his hands when he had started to cry that time, in front of everybody in the canteen.

Now Jack knew that the coarse, hard-hearted Bette had hidden another part of herself deep down somewhere. His grief had successfully released some kindness in her — a smothered mother instinct.

Jack looked across at Bette and decided it was a sheer waste of time trying to weigh people up without really knowing them well. He was discovering, as he grew older, that the top layer was no help at all when it came to character guessing.

Bette had her share of problems just like everybody else, he thought, and hers were probably mostly sexual. She was always hinting about the inadequacies of her husband. Lovemaking....the old problem that caused so much unhappiness!

Bette and her husband must be sexually unsuited, that would certainly account for her dislike of men in general, he supposed, and gave a big sigh.

"I broke one of me teeth on some brandy-snap at the Fair last year," Bette opened her mouth and displayed a broken tooth on the right-hand side of her top set.

"I'm going to see Gipsy-Rose-Lee," Iris was enthusiastic, "she's a real Romany you know. She told my pal she would get married in a few weeks....and she did."

"Huh....it's a lot of rubbish," Bette teased her. "An idiot could have told your pal she was going to get married, now couldn't they! She was about four months gone so she was bound to be getting married."

"Not if the lad had given her the Soldier's Farewell, Bette," Jack grinned at them.

"Oh, trust you to think of that, you sod. Just like a man to think of that, isn't it, Iris?"

"Yes, you rotten thing, Jack. And anyway, he wasn't a soldier, and he did marry her, so Gipsy-Rose-Lee was right. And I don't think the gipsy could tell she was....er....you know, having one, because my pal had ever such a loose coat on. You couldn't tell if you didn't know."

"Is it nearly tea-time?," Jack looked at the factory clock at the end of the room, "I can't spit a tanner." He lost interest in the conversation and the faces of his dead boys haunted him again.

★ ★ ★ ★ ★ ★

"Are you sure you don't mind me going down the Fair with the lads from work?" Jack fiddled with his tie then checked in the mirror again.

"I've told you, Jack, I'm not bothered at all about going. I'll come with you tomorrow with Alex, but I hate crowds you know that, and it'll be packed solid tonight seeing as everybody's been paid today."

"I shan't be too late then. We're going on Hyson Green for a couple of drinks first, but I should be back about eleven. I'll try and win you a coconut." He bent down and gave her a kiss on the cheek. "You're sure you don't mind then?"

"No....I'm going to listen to the wireless and finish knitting this jumper for Alex. Don't have too much to drink if you're going on a roundabout 'else you'll be sick," she fussed. "And mind out for pickpockets."

Jack closed the door behind him and stepped out into a damp, misty evening.

★ ★ ★ ★ ★ ★

She was on time — waiting near the gas-lamp on the corner of Hartley Road — near the Sweet-factory as planned. Jack walked towards her and tried not to hurry too much.

Her hair was brushed loose and in the gentle light from the gas-lamp, it reminded Jack of red and gold lace.

He took hold of her arm and pointed across the road.

"We'll walk down to that pub, over the other side of Bobbers Mill Bridge. Nags Head it's called and there shouldn't be anybody we know in there, they'll all be at the Fair tonight."

Iris nodded and Jack could see that she felt uncomfortable.

"There's no harm in it, Iris. Just a couple of drinks and a quiet talk, away from all that noise in the factory. And I've got to talk to somebody 'else I'll go mad."

—65—

He pointed to the church on the corner of Bentinck Road.

"I used to go to St. Michael's when I was a little lad." He sighed and looked up at the steeple. "It seems years-and-years ago since I was a little lad."

"Where did you used to live before you were married?" Iris was still shy and uneasy.

"I was born in Palin Street. You know, back of Bentinck School. Lived there right up until getting married. Lived on Independent Street ever since."

"That name always makes me laugh," Iris relaxed a little bit. "Isn't it a funny name for a street?"

"Yes, I suppose it is," Jack thought about it. "Some of the bus-conductors call it Well-Off Street, you know. When they pull up at the bus-stop near Jackie Pownall's junk shop, they shout 'anybody for Well-Off Street'. I think it was quite posh some years ago, but nobody's posh now. There's no money to throw around nowdays, is there! It's not a bit posh now."

"Oh I don't know, Jack. It's a lot better than some places. I was born down the Meadows and some of the houses were awful down there. And we used to have some terrible flooding. Our cellar used to be full of dirty water and smelled awful, some winters. That's why mam and dad moved to Churchfield Lane. Have you got any garden, Jack? I love nice gardens."

"Little bit at the back of the house. I grow a few vegetables but it's mostly flowers. Vera likes plenty of colour to look at. We've got Lupins, Lilies-of-the Valley, Sun-flowers, Snap-dragons, you name it we've got them. And Vera buys packets of seeds from Woolworths every spring and sets them all over the place."

"I'll bet it looks lovely in the height of summer," Iris looked into his eyes for a brief moment. "I love gardens....I could cry when I look at a beautiful garden. My dad's got an allotment — down at the side of the railway-station in Sodom — but we haven't got a proper garden at home — only postage-stamp size at the back and front. But the allotment is ever so big. Dad used to take me to his allotment every Sunday morning during the summertime before I left school, and I loved it. Picking eating apples, and pears and blackberries; rhubarb and gooseberries for pies."

They reached Gregory Boulevard and Jack ushered her across the road. A steady stream of people passed by, all on their way to the Goose Fair.

"I wish I could take you to the Fair, Iris. But I daren't chance it. Somebody'd be bound to see us."

"Oh, I don't mind, Jack. I'm going down with my pal tomorrow night. Saturday's best anyway, there's more atmosphere."

"You'll get off with lots of boys I should think," Jack tried not to look jealous. "I always used to go looking for girls on the Saturday night."

The atmosphere between them was getting more relaxed. Conversation light and flippant. Jack felt like a schoolboy again and for the first time since his children's deaths, the melancholy lifted ever so slightly and instead, exciting guilt took its place.

The smoke-room was empty, Jack pointed to a table near the fire-place. "What would you like to drink, love?"

"Er....bottle of light-ale please."

"Sure you wouldn't like a nice drop of port? It's a bit nippy tonight."

"Well all right then....but I'm not very used to drinking. My dad would go mad if he knew I was in a pub. I'm not used to drinking."

"Just have the one then and make it last." Jack went for the drinks. They sipped their drinks and got to know one another through polite questioning.

"Are your mam and dad both alive, Jack?"

"No, my mam died when I was nine and then my dad died when I'd only been married for a few months. Is your mam still alive?"

"Oh yes, I'm very lucky. And they're both ever so good to me, except my dad is a bit strict, like I was telling you just now."

"Has your dad got a job?"

"Yes, he's a dray-man at Shipstones Brewery. And my mam takes in sewing. She's ever so good — makes nearly all my clothes."

The landlord of the public house entered the room carrying a packet of spills and after lighting the fire turned to talk to them, "Nights are drawing in now, aren't they?" He nodded to Iris. "Evening Miss, have you been down the Fair then?"

"Not yet," she answered him then blushed and looked down at the lino on the floor, "I'm going down tomorrow."

"They've got some new-fangled machine 'as shakes yer insides out. My two gels had a go and they reckoned they loved it. Young 'uns nowadays, you're a damn sight dafter than we ever was."

He poked at the fire and cherry flames writhed in-and-out of the shiny black coal.

"There you are, Sir. Soon warm yer cockles." He winked at Jack before going back to his bar.

Jack took hold of Iris' hand and squeezed it.

"I like you a lot, you know that don't you!"

Iris looked embarrassed and picked up her glass of port and sipped at it for something to do.

"I know you're only just seventeen," Jack continued and still held her hand, "but I can't stop thinking about you."

"I don't think you should talk like that, Jack." Iris moved her hand away and fiddled with the top button of her coat. "I only said I'd come out for a drink and a talk. You....you are a married man."

"All right....I know I am....and there's no harm in me, honestly. I'm not going to get hold of you or anything like that," Jack picked up his pint of mild. "But I do like you a lot, I can't help that, can I!"

Iris nodded her head and looked pleased.

"It's been terrible at home since the....since the boys drowned," Jack continued. "It's just like living with a zombie, living with Vera. She won't take an interest in anything. All except for Alex that is. I dread to think what she'll be like when it's time for him to go to school. She never lets him out of her sight. And she's spoiling him to death. Everything has to revolve around Alex. Don't get me wrong, Iris....I love the lad very much....but it does get on my nerves at times. I may as well not live there for all the notice Vera takes of me. And we're....we're not like man and wife anymore. It really is getting me down."

Iris took hold of his hand and moved closer, concern showing on her face.

"It has been a terrible time for you, Jack. A really terrible time. I don't think I could have lived through it all. And you must expect it to have affected Vera an awful lot."

Jack sighed and nodded, he reached inside his jacket pocket for a packet of cigarettes. He offered the packet to Iris who declined and said, "Oh, my dad would go mad if he caught me smoking. He's a bit old-fashioned about things like that. He says it looks ever so common for a woman to smoke."

"And he's quite right, Iris," Jack lit his cigarette. "It wouldn't suit you at all, you're much too ladylike. But I thought seeing as you were surrounded by them all day long, you might be tempted to have a crafty smoke now-and-then."

"You've never seen me smoking in the canteen," Iris answered, "and I hate the way all the clothes I go to work in smell of tobacco." She laughed and the sound made Jack's heart beat faster for some inexplicable reason.

"My mam says that dad and me are a right smelly pair. I smell of tobacco all the time and dad smells of beer. Oh, but you should see his horses. They're big and daft and everybody feeds them crusts. Dad loves them and talks to them just like they were his children."

"Your dad must be a very strong man, lugging those great big beer-barrels about all day long."

Oh yes he is," Iris finished her port, "but he's a very gentle man in his ways. A bit old-fashioned, but he's a lovely dad."

"I'll fetch you another port," Jack reached for her empty glass.

"I don't think I ought to," Iris giggled, "I'm not used to shorts, only shandies, and if my dad finds out I've been in a pub he'll go mad."

"Where did you say you were going then?" Jack picked up the glass anyway and finished his own drink.

"I said I was going to the pictures with my pal."

"Just have one more and you can make it last a long time. Another one won't hurt you, I'm sure."

"All right then, but only one more," Iris fumbled inside her handbag. "I've got some Mint Imperials in here somewhere. I'll have to suck a couple before I go home."

An old man shuffled into the smoke-room and sat down, with his pint of mild, at the table on the opposite side of the fire. Half an hour later four young men bustled in and talked loudly about the Fair.

After nine o'clock the room began to fill up but luckily the other drinkers were all strangers to Jack and Iris.

The room grew warmer and the conversation and laughter louder. Jack felt relaxed and, for the first time in ages, happy. People were smiling at him; he was warm and less tensed up; and in the company of a pretty girl who seemed interested in him and liked him.

Iris seemed different to the girl she appeared to be at work. She was a little unsure of herself when away from the factory and the other girls. Same old mystery, thought Jack, you've got to peel off all those layers before you can find out what's really there.

He had never found out what Vera was all about. And now, sadly, the rift between them had grown too big and he didn't care. He pondered over the fantasies he had had about Iris all those months ago when she had been flirting with him, leading him on. The way he had imagined making love to her on those black satin sheets and what she would expect from him in return. To totally possess him.

Iris crossed one leg over the other and undid all the buttons on her coat. "Getting warm, isn't it!", her cheeks were a pretty rose pink and her eyes had the look of a contented leopardess. "Must be the port."

Jack felt the river begin to flow through his veins then surge and pound inside his brain. My God, she's beautiful, he thought, I don't think I would mind her possessing me and it wouldn't take very long either. He looked at her breasts. She's already bewitched me, he decided.

"What did you do before you came to work at the factory?" Jack noticed the daintiness of her hands, just like a lady's hands, he thought, not at all suitable for working on machinery.

"I helped my uncle Tom on his stall down Sneinton Market. He's got a pot-stall down there."

"I can't imagine you as a barrow-girl," Jack teased her, "did you shout all that 'I'm not going to ask you two shillings' or 'I'm not asking one-and-six and not even a shilling'. Did you have to do that?"

"No," she laughed with him, "uncle Tom did all that. I sold pots for him and did most of the wrapping up. We used to do a lot of travelling as well. Sometimes we went to the 'Potteries' in his lorry, to pick the pots up from the factories. We had to get up ever so early so that we could get back and set the stall up ready for half-past-eight."

"I've always wanted to do something like that — be my own boss. I'd like to work outside....I hate being cooped up in a factory."

"It's not all that marvellous, Jack. I worked for my uncle as soon as I left school when I was fourteen and it was hard work I can tell you. We travelled to other markets as well, when we'd finished down Sneinton at dinner-time. We used to keep working right up till nine o'clock and in the winter it was freezing cold. I was glad to get a job inside — the work at the factory is a lot better. And it's fairly secure, isn't it? We're very lucky I think, and I get two shillings rise twice a year and the bonus every March. I think the idea of the bonus is marvellous. It's like having your money saved up for you, in a bank. I think we're both very lucky to have such good jobs when you look at all those people in the queues every morning, waiting to see if there's any work going. I wouldn't have stood a chance of being set on if my dad hadn't got a pal in the offices. He went to school with dad, down the Meadows, and he promised to see what he could do about a job for me. I would have loved to work in the offices, you can really get on in life if you get in there. Still, I'm not grumbling,

I get another two shillings rise soon."

The port had made her talkative, she was completely at ease with Jack.

"Well I don't care what you say, Iris," Jack lit another cigarette. "I'd still like to be my own boss. Secure or not, if I could make enough money to keep Vera and the lad, I should pack my job in straight away." He shrugged his shoulders, "But you have to have some capital, something to get you started, so it looks like I'll be a machine-driver till I die."

A bell rang, the landlord shouted 'Time Gentlemen Please' and the evening was forced to its ending.

It was much colder when Jack and Iris ventured out from the warmth and friendliness of the Nags Head.

Jack smiled and said, "I'll take you to the end of Churchfield Lane, then I'll walk back up Alfreton Road. Have you enjoyed yourself this evening?"

"Yes, I have," Iris replied, "it's been lovely." She sorted about inside her handbag. "Got to suck my Mint Imperials now and tell a few fibs to my mam and dad. But it's been worth it, Jack. I like going in pubs, the people are so friendly. I can't see any harm in my going for a couple of drinks. And anyway....I'll soon be eighteen."

"Steady on," Jack laughed, "you've only just turned seventeen."

"I could pass for eighteen though, couldn't I!"

Jack looked at the innocent face, at the blush of excitement on her cheeks, the mischief lighting up her eyes. "Yes," he replied, then thought sadly, 'I wish I could remember what it felt like to be so young.' Her innocence and youth suddenly made him feel shy and very sad. After giving her a kiss on the cheek he left her at the end of Churchfield Lane. He could smell the sweetness of her minted breath all the way home.

★ ★ ★ ★ ★ ★

"Had a good time, but I didn't win you a coconut," he said to Vera, then washed and went upstairs to bed.

Vera knitted one — pearled one to the end of the row, then put down her knitting and did likewise.

Jack set the alarm for a quarter-to-seven. "There's a bit of overtime going in the morning, Vera. May as well get some in while it's going."

Vera said, "Umm," turned her back on him and was silent.

Jack pulled the bedclothes over his head, smiled, and thought, talk about all-the-fun-of-the-fair. If Vera found out where I'd been she'd go mad.

He fell asleep thinking about Iris' eyes. Those eyes that looked like a contented leopardess'.

★ ★ ★ ★ ★ ★ ★ ★ ★ ★ ★

CHAPTER FOURTEEN

"I just don't know what we're going to do about our Vera," Maisie draped the freshly ironed shirt over the clothes-horse and reached for a pinafore. She ironed the pinafore absentmindedly and repeated, "I just don't know, Nell. She's not the same girl. You can't do anything with her at all."

Nellie stared at the iron going up-and-down and said quietly, "Nothing 'as you can do, Maisie. It'll take a very long time for her to get over it. I reckon it's far worse than losing yer husband, to lose your kiddie. And to lose two at once....well you just can't imagine it, can you!"

Maisie stopped ironing and looked at her friend.

"I saw it in the tea-cups, you know. I saw the water a couple of times but I never thought...." she continued with the ironing and a black heaviness descended over the room.

"Do you know, Maisie, only a few more weeks and it'll be Christmas," Nellie changed the subject and looked at the clock on the mantlepiece. "Mr. Davenport's a bit late, isn't he! Perhaps he's taking extra orders for Christmas!"

Maisie also looked at the clock.

"He'll be here in a minute-or-two. Never has any time off. All the years I've known him he's never had any time off." She folded the pinafore in half. "I see you've got yourself tarted up for him again," she chuckled, "had your curlers in all night again, have you?"

Nellie patted the waves at the front of her hair.

"I've joined a Christmas-club. I'm going to have a Eugene perm. It's going to cost me eight-and-sixpence, but the hairdresser says it'll last for months and months. And it'll even keep in curl when the weather's damp and rainy. Eh....", she paused and looked very pleased with herself, "I've put a deposit on a new frock."

"My word, you are splashing out on yourself, Nell. I can smell summat in the wind. What's going off....come on now....tell me."

"Nothing's going off," Nellie grinned at her, "I just thought 'as I'd like to smarten myself up a bit. And seeing as our Tim got on as an apprentice at the bike factory, and since the washing and ironing comes in regular from the butcher's wife, I'm a bit better off than I was."

"What's this frock like then, you've ordered?", Maisie was interested.

"Oh, wait till you see it, Maisie. I've always wanted one like it. It's got the latest padded shoulders and a frill all down the front," she pointed to her flat chest, "all down here. And it's in a lovely shade of saxe blue. It's wool, with satin on the cuffs and all on the edge of the frill."

"Huh....when you've had that perm and got done up in your new frock, you'll look like Marlene Deitrich."

"Not with my skinny legs, I won't," Nellie pulled her skirt above her knees and looked down at her legs.

The tea salesman tapped on the half open door and stepped inside the room.

"Just in time for a leg show, Mr. Davenport," Maisie chuckled and nodded towards Nellie's legs.

Bill Davenport whistled and stared at Nellie's legs, "I like a nice pair of slim legs. You look like what's her name in that film 'The Blue Angel'."

"There you are, Nell," Maisie placed the iron on a metal stand, "I was just telling her that, Mr. Davenport. Now then you two, I expect you could both fancy a nice cup of tea!" She went into the kitchen and put the kettle on the gas-stove.

"I'm a bit late this afternoon, ladies," Bill Davenport put his order-book on top of the gramophone then sat in the armchair nearest the fire and stared into the flames.

Nellie fidgeted with her fingers and looked into the kitchen at Maisie.

"Here you are, nice bit of home-made cake," Maisie cut the cake into slices, "I made it myself and there's three fresh eggs in it." She winked, "The eggs are from the Carter's house. They have them delivered from a farm up Wollaton, and they never need half as many as they order."

She looked sharply at Bill Davenport as she handed him a plate and enquired, "Feeling all right are you, Mr. Davenport? You look a bit peeky today. Aren't sickening for summat, are you?"

Nellie and Maisie both stared at him and waited for his reply.

"I may as well tell you," he shrugged his shoulders, "I've had to go to the doctors for a bit of a tonic. I've been feeling a bit run down." He stared at the floor and continued, "It'll be all round Sodom in no time. My wife's run off with another bloke."

"Oh dear!" Nellie and Maisie chorussed.

"And the awful part about it....I never suspected anything was going off. I feel a right mug I can tell you. She just said she was leaving me....right out-of-the-blue. Going to start a new life in Grantham with this bloke. And of course, since she's been gone, lots of people have told me they knew all about it. He used to go round to the house when I was on my tea rounds. He's a pork-butcher and got his staff to look after his shop, while he was messing about with my missis. He's well-off too, because he's bought a bigger shop in Grantham. That's where they're going to live....in Grantham."

"Never mind, duck," Maisie said kindly, "there's worse things than that can happen to you." She reached for a knife and spread butter on his piece of cake.

"Here you are, duck....a nice bit of best butter on your cake. You enjoy that while I go and mash the tea."

Nellie still fidgeted with her fingers and said nothing.

Once again three ordinary people, eating ordinary cake, drinking ordinary tea — but what extraordinary thoughts were they thinking!

Maisie, burdened with grief and guilt since the deaths of her beloved grandchildren.

Bill Davenport, ill with shock and worry at the departure of his wife. And Nell, looking years older than she was, worn-out with ironing and washing — scraping a living somehow — hanging on through dreams of perms and frilly frocks and a longing to be loved sometime in her life.

Maisie melted the scene back to life with the remark, "If you want any washing or ironing doing, Nell's the one to ask, aren't you, Nell?"

"Oh....er....yes," Nellie bit daintily into her piece of cake and blushed.

"And she's a beautiful little cook. Her pastry melts in your mouth." Nellie's eyes pleaded with Maisie to stop, but she need not have worried because Bill Davenport did not seem to notice Maisie's unsubtle prompting.

"It's the loneliness when you go home at night that gets you," Bill sipped at his tea. "Not so bad in the daytime when I've got my round to do. Plenty of people to talk to then. But it's in the evenings, with only the wireless for company that gets you."

"You could go to the pub, or the pictures," Maisie suggested. "We love a good picture, don't we, Nell?" She threw him a crafty feminine life line but he did not grasp it.

Nellie drained the last of her tea and pretended to be extremely interested in the tea leaves.

Bill Davenport stood up and wrote some figures in his order book.

"Thank you very much for the tea and cake. See you next week then, ladies." He tucked the book underneath his arm and stepped out on to the Avenue once again.

"I reckon that new frock and Eugene perm might just do the trick," said Maisie. "Pass me your cup and I'll have a look what the leaves say."

Nellie passed her cup and chewed on a few of the leaves, "Hurry up, Maisie, can you see 'owt?"

"Only a load of tea leaves," answered Maisie and laughed. "But that could be a good sign....if you get my meaning!"

★★★★★★★★★★★★

CHAPTER FIFTEEN

Vera wished that she could get rid of the feeling of walking through marshmallow clouds all the time. Everything seemed to be too much trouble. Shopping was a nightmare; all the remembering which food to buy and the meals needing to be cooked. She had given up dusting the furniture, and the clothes, when she had ironed them, did not look any different. Ironing seemed like such hard work so she only skimmed over the freshly washed clothes.

Rupert the cat understood how she felt and sat on her knee for hours, listening sympathetically whilst she told him all her troubles.

Alexander understood too of course, because he missed Frankie and Dougie just as much as she did, but he was too young to give her much comfort.

And Jack....Jack seemed like a stranger living in the house. He had started to go out to the pub in the evenings and she was glad because then she did not have to think of things to talk to him about when he came home from work.

She could not talk to him like she could Rupert and Alexander. Of course it was not her fault, nobody would want to talk about cigarettes and cigarette machines every night. And that was all Jack was interested in....cigarettes.

Vera looked at the Christmas tree. The smiling Father Christmas, dangling from one of the middle branches, seemed to be mocking her.

The fairy looking down from the top of the tree stared at her with painted dead eyes and yet, Vera imagined that the eyes could pierce into her thoughts, knew exactly what she was thinking. "What are you staring at", she asked the fairy, "have you seen enough?"

Christmas had come-and-gone but the tree and the paper garlands hanging from the ceiling would remain until Twelfth Night. Yesterday it had snowed, Jack had made a snowman. Today it was raining, snowmen had skulked away down 'fever-grates'.

Vera heard the laughter of her boys as they ran up the entry, dodging the rain, hungry for hot toast and freshly mashed tea.

She pulled the net curtain aside and stared out at the grey slate roofs of the houses opposite. The slates had been transformed to sparkling blocks of silver by the downpour and here and there a kitchen light shone out through the veil of rain and reminded Vera once again of a luxury liner with its port-holes and fairy-lights.

Alex, tucked up on the sofa for his afternoon nap, whimpered in his sleep. Vera turned to him, an automatic mother's reaction, and gently stroked his hair and said, "Shush....shush."

She looked at the Christmas tree once more and said to the fairy, "I'm going on that ship, you know."

"Oh, I knew that," answered the fairy, "we both knew."

Vera nodded at the painted fairy doll and the mocking Father Christmas. She checked to see if the fireguard was secure, then left the house. The rain embraced her in an ice cold shawl of tears.

★ ★ ★ ★ ★ ★

Mrs. Cohen was sitting in her usual spot near the front window, she looked up from her knitting as Vera drew level with the window. Mrs. Cohen waved and smiled but Vera did not return the smile so Mrs. Cohen banged on the window.

Vera stopped and stared at the window but did not acknowledge that she had seen Mrs. Cohen sitting there. Mrs. Cohen hurried to the front door and peered out into the rain.

"How are you, Mrs. Denbey?" She stared at Vera who only nodded her head in reply.

It was raining heavily and the wind chilling, but Vera had no umbrella, was hatless and wore only a skirt and jumper. Mrs. Cohen looked at her in astonishment. Vera was also wearing carpet slippers and her hair was hanging bedraggled, with tiny bobbles of rain hanging on the end, but she did not appear to notice that it was raining.

"What are you doing, out without your coat?" Mrs. Cohen rocked from side-to-side, arms folded across her breasts. "You'll catch your death of cold. Please, please come in for a minute and warm yourself. Are you going to the shops on Denman Street?" Mrs. Cohen held out her hands and beckoned to Vera, "Please, come on inside for a while out of the rain. I've got a nice bottle of sherry my boy sent me for Christmas. Didn't get over again this year, but he sent me plenty of food and drink. Come and have a drop of sherry."

"No time, Mrs. Cohen. I've got to get there before it sails."

"Before what sails?", Mrs. Cohen looked puzzled, "what?"

"The ship of course! The ship with all the lights shining through the port-holes. And there'll be a dance and I'll wear a long evening frock." Mrs. Cohen no longer looked puzzled — realisation showed in the expression of horror on her face. She held out her hands imploringly now and reached for Vera's hands.

Vera stepped away from her and shook her head, "I've told you....I must be there on time. We're going all over the world. We're all going this time....Jack ....Frankie....Dougie....Alex. We're all going this time."

She turned to go and said, "I've got to get there before it sails, 'else they'll go without me. They mustn't go without me this time."

"Mrs. Denbey.......!" Mrs. Cohen called after her, but the wind and rain washed the air clean of her cries.

Vera hurried round the corner on to Denman Street. The cold and rain had kept people indoors so the street was almost deserted. All the children in the neighbourhood were at school. But no-one would have taken much notice of Vera anyway, because women often nipped out to the shops without their coats, and lots of them did not bother to exchange slippers for shoes, not even when it was pouring with rain.

The wind was unpredictable and blew the curtain of rain in many directions.

Vera reached St. Peters Street and was soon at the Penny Weigh-Bridge. The River Leen rushed on its way towards the Trent — swelled by the snow and rain it gushed and gurgled like thousands of taps turned on simultaneously.

Vera stopped for a few seconds and looked over the wall at the water. "Not here, not here," she murmured, and continued walking, her head held down against the icy needles of rain.

Over Radford railway bridge and the railway station. She hesitated for a few seconds at the top of Canterbury Road then continued walking, past the large gasometers and onwards towards the tiny school-house.

As she reached the Wollaton Road School children's voices sang out; it was an old folk-song about gypsies and a lady's heart melting away like snow. Vera hesitated again, listened to the children, then continued walking.

A few more yards and she paused at a wooden gate at the end of the road. She opened the gate and walked down a path which sloped — towards the canal.

The canal water frolicked and frothed; and there was a lock-gate decorated as though for Christmas with hanging, dark green weeds and snapped off branches of trees.

Vera walked underneath the tiny hump-back bridge towards the lock-gate. She climbed onto the worn, slippery wood and peered down into the deep trough of dark swirling water.

After a while she looked into the distance and murmured, "Thank goodness it isn't here yet." She spoke out aloud, addressing the water, "I hope it gets here before it turns too dark, 'else they won't be able to see me."

She sat down on the lock and dangled her feet in the water. Her slippers came off and danced about on top of the water before disappearing into the cold depths, but she did not notice.

Vera put her hands up to her eyes, shielding them from the pouring rain, and looked out to sea for the luxury liner.

★★★★★★★★★★★★

CHAPTER SIXTEEN

Independent Street reminded Jack of a gigantic Swiss weather-vane. On fine summer evenings out came the people, children and dogs. Women sitting in doorways on chairs or perching on steps; men in crouching positions sitting beside them, relaxing after a hard day's slog in the factories; they rolled up shirt sleeves and let trouser braces dangle.

In the wintertime doors remained shut and old women like Mrs. Cohen sat at windows and watched and waited; for other people's excitement and their own deaths.

The children always ventured out — children glad to escape from the discipline inflicted on them by parents and school-teachers. Noisy lads playing football, jumping on-and-off garden walls, running up-and-down entries, spirit-tapping on doors, and whistling and shouting after giggling girls.

And then there were the dogs — nipping out for a quick round of the lamp-posts and a few sniffs at the cellar-grates which they also liked to pee down.

Jack turned the corner and there it was — his street — heralding a fine, warm evening. The street was alive with vitality and colour despite the shortage of money and employment.

"Ow do, Jack. How's the missis keeping now then? Better is she?"

"Did you back that one I gen yer on Sat'day, Jack? Went like the wind din't it. I gorra double up. Won over five quid."

"Ah....and he spent most of it on ale, Jack. Boozed-up all weekend."

"Any jobs going in your department, Jack? I'm on me uppers now."

"Oh thanks, Jack. You're a pal. 'Ent 'ad a fag all day. I'll pay yer back when I get fixed up with a job."

"Ah....when Nelson gets his bleddy eye back....that'll be, Jack."

Jack walked towards his home and looked all around him. Boys crouched over holes in the cobbled road, with crooked forefingers they tried to win a blood-alley or an eye-of-the-moon marble from their pals.

Little girls skipped using pieces of washing-line or, if they were lucky, real skipping-ropes with painted wooden handles; high pitched voices singing in monotone the tunes taught to them by elder sisters and mothers.

"My mother said, I never should, play with the gipsies in the wood.
If I did, she would say, naughty girl to disobey.
Disobey....disobey....naughty girl to disobey."

"On the mountains stands a lady, who she is I do not know
All she wants is gold and silver, all she wants is a nice young man.
So call in my Lucy dear, Lucy dear, Lucy dear,
So call in my Lucy dear, while I go out to play."

Toddlers swayed all over the place, going down like fat skittles; mothers kissed scraped knees better, rubbed lard on bruised foreheads, and hugged tear-stained faces to pinafored bosoms.

For a few moments Jack felt an overpowering feeling of warmth towards his neighbours and then sighed as he thought about their lives, the way they settled for almost nothing. Jack still longed for excitement, travel and escape although he had almost resigned himself to living forever in Independent Street, until they carried him out in a wooden overcoat, as he called it. He reached the corner of Dennison Street. Ah well, he thought, things could be much worse. Vera seemed a lot better; nursed back to health and reality by the wonderful staff at the Mapperley hospital — the one where they locked you up — she was almost ready for coming home again they had told him.

Maisie had been marvellous too, offering to care for Alex until Vera was well enough to come home, she had given Jack a temporary bachelor life once again.

Jack put his key in the lock and entered the silent house. Rupert jumped down from the top of the sideboard, arched his back, yawned and sidled up to Jack for some attention.

"Let's see what we've got for your dinner," Jack rubbed the cat's head. "Better make the most of it hadn't we, old lad. Your mam'll be coming home soon....there'll be no more sleeping on the sideboard then. Now then," he looked in the cupboard at the side of the fireplace, "if I have sardines-on-toast for my tea you can share them with me." Rupert purred agreement and tried to leg Jack over.

After Jack had eaten his tea he took a carrier-bag from the sideboard and put clean underclothes, razor and stick of shaving soap into it.

On Thursday evenings Jack went to the Boden Street public-baths for his weekly soak. He would have preferred to have his bath at home but it took such a long while for the water in the copper to heat up and it was so time consuming having to get the bath down from its nail on the wall in the backyard and then clean it down so, Jack went to Boden Street to enjoy the luxury of the hospital-type baths with the endless supply of hot water, the skin-burning hot water.

Jack checked the time — he was meeting Iris at half-past-eight. They had arranged to go for a walk and he decided to take her to the fields near the railway lines, just past Radford Pit over the other side of the railway-bridge. It was difficult to find secluded places, hideaways where nobody would know them, especially now the evenings stayed light until well after nine o'clock.

How long had it been now, Jack paused for a moment, deep in thought. He had been seeing Iris after work since last October — since the Goose Fair when he had first taken her to the Nags head for a drink. And the relationship had turned out exactly how Jack had forecast to himself. He had become obsessed with her and she had led him on, letting him go just so far, driving him crazy with longing then snap....putting the shutters up. Even after the awful time when Vera's mind had cracked up, because of the boys' deaths, Jack still could not stop seeing Iris. In fact he needed her more, she was a comfort, someone to talk to, someone nice to look at and hold.

Jack hurried into the kitchen with the carrier-bag, reached up to the shelf above the sink and said to the cat, "Nearly forgot my shaving brush." He put the brush into the bag and left the house whistling a tune.

★★★★★★

Iris dangled her fingers into the water and looked down, tried to see her reflection in the dark green. The tiny waterfall further up the river gurgled and splashed then the water it sent down divided into two for a stretch before curving round and joining forces again and flowing underneath the bridge at the end of St. Peters Street, dying to get to the river Trent.

"If we're going for a walk near the railway bridge we'd better keep an eye out for my dad," Iris looked worried, "he said he might go down to his allotment tonight. He's been asking me a lot of questions lately....about where I'm going and who with. I'm not sure, Jack, but I think he suspects something's going off."

"We'll keep this side of the allotments then," Jack tugged at the brim of his trilby hat and then took hold of Iris' hand. "Come on, let's go and get some nice fresh air into our lungs." He breathed deeply and stuck out his chest.

"What!" Iris stood up, "fill them with the smell from the pit and cigarette factory do you mean!" She grinned at him.

"It smells lovely near the allotments," Jack breathed deeply again, "all the hedgerows and vegetation. Come on," he hurried her along, "let's find somewhere nice and quiet. I want to give you a nice big kiss."

They walked up the path flanked on either side by hedgerows adorned with tiny pink, and white roses. Nestling at the bottom of the hedgerows were nettles, dock leaves, dandelions and pretty purple willow herb.

Before they had reached the railway bridge a train screamed a warning of its approach then left a grey haze of smoke hanging suspended over the bridge and gravelled path which led up to it.

"I always feel excited when I see a train and smell the smoke from the engine," Jack looked after the train until the last carriage had gone from view. "I start thinking about all those people on the train....who are they....where are they off to....who are they going to meet....!"

"It makes me feel like that as well," Iris looked over the side of the bridge then stood on tiptoe and peered down at the railway lines. "I've only been on trains to Matlock and Skegness. I'd like to travel first class and have a real leather suitcase with my initials on the side. And go away for two whole weeks and have lots of money to spend on daft things."

Jack nodded agreement and answered, "Oh yes, and have a three-course meal in the dinner-car, with waiters rushing up to serve you and calling you sir. Then strolling back to your first-class carriage and smoking a big fat cigar."

"And get off the train at London and have a porter carry your suitcase to a taxi," Iris was enjoying the fantasy.

"Yes, then catch another train — a boat train. Get on board a ship going to some foreign place," Jack sighed and looked at Iris' face. Her eyes sparkled with good health and the corners of her mouth, turned charmingly upwards by a smile, made her look innocent and even more alluring.

"I don't know what you see in me, Iris," Jack pulled her close to him and rubbed his hands gently up and down her back. He looked all around to see if they were still alone. "A married man," he continued, "years older than you, and no money to brag about. I don't know what you see in me," he repeated and buried his head into her hair. The exciting scent of Evening-in-Paris perfume which she had sprinkled on to her hair aroused him and he pressed himself closer to her and kissed her on the mouth.

Iris pushed him away and whispered, "Now you mustn't start that again, Jack. What if somebody who knows us sees us!"

"Let's find somewhere sheltered then," Jack coaxed her down the other side of the railway bridge, towards the lane leading to the allotments. Iris had started to let him feel her breasts and, at the thought of it, Jack began to feel anxious and breathless as though the most important thing in the world to him was to feel inside her blouse and fondle the firm, young, tantalising mounds; made more exciting because they were forbidden.

Someone from one of the allotments had lit a fire — the smell of garden rubbish, blending with the train and vegetation smells, reminded Jack of his childhood for some inexplicable reason. It had a peculiar affect upon him and he felt a sadness creeping inside his chest — it mingled with the sexual longing and surged through his body.

"Let's find a garden where they've not locked the gate," he had a caressing, gentle tone in his voice. "Come on, love, let's find somewhere." They walked for a while longer, Jack pushed a gate open.

"Here's one....come on."

Iris followed him into the allotment and sat down on the jacket Jack had spread on the ground, in a corner hidden away behind a greenhouse full of ripening tomatoes.

It was beginning to get dark and the fading light and quietness helped them in their desire to be hidden and completely alone.

Iris sat upright her hands resting on her lap. Jack put his arm around her waist and kissed her very gently on the cheek. She responded by putting her arms around his neck and kissing him on the lips.

Jack felt the sadness inside his chest melting away and instead, the river began its gurgling journey through the veins inside his head. He imagined Iris naked on the black satin sheets and his breathlessness returned.

He leaned against Iris and she fell back onto the jacket, her eyes concentrating on Jack's face, she smiled at him in a grown-up, all knowing kind of way.

Jack undid the buttons of her blouse and felt inside, his fingers gently caressing her soft, warm breasts.

"Will you let me do it tonight, Iris?" his voice was pleading, "please love, just this once. I won't hurt you. You'll love it, I know you will."

Iris closed her eyes, put her hands on his, then drew them away from her breasts and answered, "No....it's still light. I'm shy....I've told you....I'm too shy to let you do that. I don't want you to see me, not when it's light." She paused and added, "And anyway, I don't want you to."

"Yes you do," Jack put his hands back inside her blouse, "your breasts are beautiful. You should be proud to show them off. You've no need to hide them. They are really beautiful." He was finding it difficult to speak properly. "I don't want to make love to you....you know that, don't you! And anyway....you won't let me, will you? I just want to kiss your breasts. Please Iris....please....just this once." He kissed her throat then edged his way further down towards her breasts. "I'll keep my eyes closed. I promise to keep my eyes closed all the time if you'll let me." His mouth ventured lower. He undid the tiny rubber buttons on her liberty bodice then pressed her down — she found it difficult to struggle against him.

Iris tried to push him away but did not really put too much effort into her struggling. After a while she relaxed a little and put her hands on his back.

Jack's love play had all the well practised expertise of the married man and Iris soon abandoned herself to the new found delight.

The last of the light faded and Jack was sure he would have remained at her breasts all night if Iris had not pushed him away and said, "It's late, Jack. I'll have to go now. My dad'll go mad when he sees what time it is."

Iris fastened her blouse, took a comb from her handbag and started to tidy her hair. Jack sat up and lit a cigarette. He looked at Iris' hair flowing in red-gold waves over her shoulders, catching beams of light from the moon which had just won a battle with a cloud, and thought that if he lived forever he would never see anything more beautiful. More than anything else he wanted to make love to her, be part of her body, and take pleasure in thrilling and pleasing her. But it will have to be taken very slowly, he thought, like winning the confidence of a shy fawn or delicate exotic bird. I can wait, he puffed at his cigarette, and thought about her breasts.

"You think I'm awful, don't you! Letting you do that! I'm not coming down the allotments again, Jack. I feel awful letting you do that. It's the very last time....I mean it, Jack. I feel ever so cheap."

Jack smiled to himself all the way home. How clever and practical women were — even the seventeen year olds. They didn't feel cheap at all. Not normal, healthy women didn't. They loved you to fondle them, it made them feel powerful, the hold they could have on a man if they wanted. Look how I've been pleading and acting like a young daft lad, he mused, just so's I could kiss Iris' breasts. And she loved it, lay there as quiet as a mouse, loved every minute of it, then pretended she was only doing it to please me. Wait till she gives in completely, she'll not be able to keep away from me then, not once she's had a taste.

Jack let Rupert out into the night after giving him a saucer of milk and said, "I hope you have better luck than me, old lad."

Jack lay on top of his bed, because the air had turned humid, and thought about the last few hours. He did not feel guilty but the feeling he did have was not pleasant. A cross between miserable and bewilderment. Vera would be home shortly and then he would have to start lying again everytime he wanted to go out. And it was beginning to get difficult at work. Bette had dropped a few hints although he wasn't sure whether she knew about Iris and him. And somehow, seeing Iris all day long seated at his machine, the novelty had gone out of their romance. If only I could get another job away from the cigarette factory, he blew cigarette smoke towards the window, my life's all mixed up. All my problems would be solved if I could be completely engrossed in something I really liked. Get my own business going and travel around a bit.

The light from the gas lamp on the corner of the street flickered a dancing mural on the walls. Jack stubbed out his cigarette and settled down to sleep hoping that his dreams would not hold as many problems for him as reality did.

★★★★★★★★★★★★

CHAPTER SEVENTEEN

Everything in the house was the same but, paradoxically, the surroundings seemed totally alien to Vera. In the hospital she had remembered the room as it had been on the cold winter's day when she had left it, but now the Christmas decorations had been put away, there was no fire burning and no toys lying about. Vera felt as if she had come back to a stranger's house.

Maisie had nipped out to the shops and left Vera to adapt herself to being home again. Vera stared at the empty hearth and sighed.

Maisie had travelled on the two buses with her, back from the hospital. Jack had offered to fetch her out but half-a-day's pay was precious so Alf had volunteered to stay up on his return from his night-shift, and look after Alex until Maisie had seen to things at Independent Street.

Rupert had not forgotten her — he rubbed against Vera's legs then padded up-and-down on her lap as soon as she sat down on the sofa.

Vera stroked his head and thought and thought, arranging her mind into some sort of pattern. What had they said at the hospital? First of all, when you were unhappy, you had to look back all the time and face whatever it was that had made you so miserable. Then, once you had been able to do that, you had to concentrate on the present and plan for the future.

She made a mental list of the debit side of her life. Her two beautiful boys both drowned and gone forever; the aborted child which she knew she had been punished for; lack of money and....she came to a full stop and could not think of anything else. Now, what had the doctor said? The first things on her list she couldn't do anything about. Nothing could ever change death. So, she had to close that episode of her life, like coming to the end of a chapter in a book, she had to turn the page and carry on.

But perhaps the money part could be resolved! The secret was never to give up, like she had done all those months ago. She would try and find some part-time work. Washing, ironing, or an evening picture usherette; anything that would keep her mind occupied.

The doctor had also said she must not smother Alex with too much attention. He could never be a substitute for his two brothers. It was very bad for both her and him, they had told her at the hospital. She would stunt the growth of his personality if she continued to cling to him. Vera had to get things into the proper departments of life, that way both mother and son would benefit. And anyway, he would soon be ready for school. That's the time when you really lose them, she thought sadly, when the teachers grabbed a hold on them; when they developed friendships with other boys and later on, girls.

She lifted the net curtains to one side and pressed her face against the window. It was a shimmering-pearl-of-a-day; everything transformed into something better by the sunshine.

Vera told herself that maybe it was symbolic, all that sunshine and warmth on her first day home. She stepped out of the back kitchen and walked down the path at the side of the tiny patch of garden.

"Ey up me duck, how yer going on then!" a neighbour hanging out washing in the garden three doors away took clothes pegs from her mouth and greeted Vera. "Did you like them flowers we sent you? Bert cut the best 'uns for you. You're looking well, Vera."

A man looked out of the backyard of the house, his wife nodded towards Vera and said to him, "Here's Vera. I was just asking her if she liked them flowers we sent her."

"Ey up, love....nice to see you home again. We've missed you....and the little lad. I've missed the little bogger bumping up me legs with his scooter. You liked the flowers then, did you! Couldn't send any chocolates or 'owt like that, I'm still on the dole. I thought about robbing a bank, but I couldn't afford to buy a gun. Are yer mashing then, Annie? Get Vera a nice cup of tea. Always fancy a cup can't we, Vera?" he grinned at her.

Vera smiled at Bert and Annie. It had been worrying her that neighbours would feel uncomfortable knowing that she had been in Mapperley, but Annie and Bert seemed just the same as before. Concentrate on the present and plan for the future, she told herself, then walked over to the garden-wall and waited for her tea.

After a few minutes Maisie walked up the entry with a carrier-bag full of groceries. She shouted to the three tea drinkers, "Any left in the pot? Can't spit a tanner."

She went up to Vera and said happily, "The butcher's sent you some spare-ribs. I went to buy that polony for yours and Jack's tea and the butcher asked after you. When I told him you'd come home, straight away he picked up his chopper and cut some ribs up. Tell her they're on me, he said, put hairs on her chest, the broth will. I said you wouldn't want hairs on your chest, but you'd enjoy the lovely spare-ribs."

"Aye aye," Bert winked at them, "you want to watch him, Vera. You know what they say about butchers don't you?"

"No, what do they say?" Maisie put the carrier-bag down on the floor and grinned at him, egging him on.

"They're never without their choppers in their hands."

Maisie laughed and Vera smiled, Bert was encouraged more.

"It's handling all that meat all day long that does it. Makes them randy as bulls."

"Is he being dirty again?" Annie returned with Maisie's cup of tea. "Who's as randy as a bull then? I'll tell you one thing girls, he's not on about hisself," Annie folded arms across her bulging-out-of-blouse bosom. "The only time he wants 'owt is when he's had some Shipstones' ale. But when he's got money for some 'Shippos' he drinks that much he forgets he wanted summat in the first place."

"Go on with yer," Bert scratched his hairy chest that was partly hidden underneath the off-white vest he was wearing, "I'm a great lover I am," he winked at Maisie and Vera again. "A woman once told me I looked like.... ooooh .... what's that bloke's name....er....? The king of Hollywood he is."

"With your hairy chest, you look more like King Kong," Annie teased him.

Everyone laughed again then Bert became serious and said, "Anyway love, 'owt you need....anything bothering you....you've only got to nip round here. Me and Annie want you to know that." He looked embarrassed and continued, "And send that young bogger of yours to see me when he gets back home 'cause I've made him a ginger-bread man out of a piece of wood."

Annie collected the cups and saucers from the top of the garden wall and added, "He has an' all. It took him ages it did. Whittling away at it for hours on end."

"Ah," Bert chuckled, "it started out a giant and finished up more like a midget."

"It's got a right ugly mug," said Annie, "it'll frighten the lad to death, it will."

"Ah, it looks just like Annie's mother," added Bert.

"Ooh, you cheeky sod," said Annie, "just for that you can wash these pots." She handed the pots to Bert then stuck more clothes-pegs into her mouth and picked a shirt from the laundry basket.

Vera decided that she loved Bert and Annie even though she did not know them very well. It's easy to love people, she thought, it didn't cost anything and didn't require any great effort. You just had to feel a certain way and it was there in plenty; to give out all over the place.

Oh, I'm really looking forward to lying in Jack's arms tonight, she thought and then felt shy. How nice it is to be back home again.

She linked arms with Maisie and said to her, "I'll come with you to get Alex, mam. Then how about going into town this afternoon? Let's go to Marks and Spencers and both buy a daft hat."

She felt the neighbours' stares, on Independent Street, would be easier to cope with if she looked smart and fashionable. Then they would see that she was completely well again — bothering to take care of herself.

She decided to have a perm as well, if Jack could afford to treat her to one.

The sun exploded into a million shafts of shimmering warmth, embracing the back-garden and the technicolor array of flowers.

"My snap-dragons have done well this year, mam," Vera nodded towards the garden, "all they need is a bit of sunshine to help them along."

"Just like us, love," answered Maisie, "all we need is a bit of sunshine now-and-then, help us get through all the rotten times eh!" She smiled at Vera. "Now then, let's put this shopping away and then we'll go and pick Alex up. I'll bet poor old Bert's dying to get to bed. Eh....I fancy a hat with a bunch of cherries at the side. What do you fancy, duck?"

★ ★ ★ ★ ★ ★ ★ ★ ★ ★ ★

CHAPTER EIGHTEEN

It had been quite a day for Maisie. She put on a clean pinafore then checked to see if the fish she was steaming for Alf's tea had been cooked enough. She called to Alf from the bottom of the stairs.

"Alf....Alfie....are you awake, love! It's nearly four."

"Right you are, be down in a few minutes," Alf answered her from the bedroom and added, "haven't had my full eight hours yet."

Maisie called back to him, "Five minutes won't make much difference to your beauty sleep. And I've got some news for you. A bit of scandal." Her voice sounded agitated, "It's about our Jack, some of it."

That'll shift him, she thought, can't resist a bit of scandal. Pretends he's not interested in other people's business, but likes a bit of scandal on the quiet.

Maisie was right — Alf was soon downstairs; tousled haired and stubbled chinned, eyes like a chinaman's, slitty and heavy with sleep.

"I don't know about scandal," said Alf as he entered the room, "a nice cup of tea, that's what I want, love." He kissed her on the cheek. "Blimey....I slept like the dead today. They kept me busy last night. Two coppers came prowling about and of course, they wanted cups of tea and a chat. They hung on and hung on, 'cause it was raining, and then one of the blokes from the paint shop reported he'd seen some youths climbing over a wall, near Lenton Boulevard entrance. I had to go traipsing all the way up there and help Frank and George to have a good look round." Alf adjusted the chord of his pyjamas and flopped into his favourite chair.

Maisie handed Alf his tea and said, "Nellie's only just gone home. You'll never guess, Alf....you'll never guess what!" She poured tea for herself and sat down on the ottoman. "Mr. Davenport's asked Nell to go out with him, tomorrow night," her eyes shone, sparkling with pleasure at the news, "he's taking her to the pictures."

"Blimey....and you made me get out of bed just for that!" Alf pretended not to be interested, "what's exciting about that then? I thought you were going to say he was taking her to Monte Carlo or summat like that. Pictures is now't."

"No," Maisie smiled at him and went coy, "but it can lead to other things can't it! Look what happened when you took me to the pictures."

Alf looked puzzled and replied, "I can't remember 'owt happening. Oh yes....I do remember now. You cried and blew your nose in my best hankie 'cause an orphan died in that daft picture at the Lenos," he teased her.

"It wasn't a daft picture and I didn't mean that, and you know it. What I meant was, it could lead to a big romance. Could lead up to a wedding if we give them a bit of encouragement. I've never seen Nell looking so radiant. I reckon it was her perm that did the trick."

"Huh, you do say some funny things, Maisie. He's not going to spend all his time looking at her blooming hair."

"No, but men like a bit of glamour and Nell's tried very hard to look something like. And anyway, apart from her hair, she'll make him a good wife. She's a lovely little cook, and knitter. And look how she makes her money spin out! And Nell's not afraid of hard work. I've known her sit up till three in the morning putting hair-nets on cards. And she's got up at half-past six the same morning and gone scrubbing."

Alf was serious now, he nodded his head and answered, "You're right, Maisie....she's a good 'un. I hope they make a go of it. She needs a bloke to look after her and I like that Bill. Not much personality, but he looks a good steady sort of bloke. Perhaps that's why his missis boggered off! Wanted somebody with a bit more go in him!"

"I've got some more news," Maisie looked serious and fiddled with the tassles on the end of the chenille tablecloth, "not very nice I'm afraid, Alf. I'm ever so worried about it in fact."

"Come on then....tell me so's I can worry about it as well," Alf's mouth quivered mischievously; he reached on the mantlepiece for his pipe.

"I suppose I've got time to light me pipe before you get round to telling me! Hurry up, Maisie, the suspense's killing me." He thrust a spill into the fire and lit the tobacco, then sucked and puffed sending smoke spiralling into the air.

"Our Jack's seeing a young girl." Maisie delivered the news like a tragedy queen at the Theatre Royal. "He's been seen walking arm-in-arm with her, over near the waterfall, down by the side of Radford Folly."

"Oh, come on now," Alf puffed on his pipe, "who's told you that load of rubbish? He was probably walking by the side of her in his dinner time. They all go for a stroll when they come out of the canteen, 'specially when it's nice weather. It's a nice walk down by the side of the Leen and the allotments. She probably works in his department....there's no crime in walking with one of your workmates in your dinner time."

"It wasn't at dinner time, it was at night and he was all over her. She's only a young girl, about sixteen, and she's got long red hair. She was all over him as well."

"And who's told you all this then?"

"It was Mrs. Greenwood from off Trafalgar Street. Her Audrey works in the same department as Jack and it was her who saw them down the allotments one night."

"You're not going to tell your Vera, are you, Maisie? She's getting over everything lovely now. If she finds out about it, it'll put her back in the Big-house. Leave things alone, let him have his fussy out. He'll soon get fed up, when he's had his fussy out."

"Oh no, I'm not saying anything to Vera," Maisie bit on the inside of her left cheek, nervous chewing of soft flesh, a habit she had acquired when threatened with a good hiding in her schooldays. "What bothers me is if he does anything foolish."

"Huh, going about with a young gel's being foolish if you ask me. I blame the gel more than Jack. She wants her arse smacking, she does. She must know Jack's married."

"I meant put her in the family way, that sort of foolishness. Do you think it might help if you had a word with Jack? You know, tell him it's all over Radford about him and the girl. That might bring him to his senses," Maisie chewed faster on her left cheek. "I don't know, Alf....there's always summat to worry about in't there? No sooner do you get rid of one worry, then another one crops up to take its place. If our Vera gets to know about this little lot if could turn her completely. I don't know whatever Jack's thinking of."

"You know Maisie, in a way I can understand Jack's falling for this gel. No, don't chime in, just let me tell you what I think. He's had a terrible, terrible time lately....with the lads er...." he paused and stared at the floor, "....and then your Vera breaking down. Well....some nice young gel gets a bit friendly towards him, leads him on a bit, and Bobs-your-uncle." He smiled at Maisie and continued, "Don't worry too much about it, love. He'll not leave your Vera or 'owt like that. He wouldn't have the heart....no man would not after what she's been through. I vote we keep quiet and stay out of it. We'll pretend we don't know 'owt about it."

"Yes, all right then, Alf. That'll be the best thing."

"In a few week's time it'll all be forgotten. It'll be old news. The gel will have chucked him for some young lad. They're not daft you know, nowdays they're not. She won't hang around for long when she sees Jack's sticking to Vera."

"The only problem is if he gets her in the family way." Maisie sighed a sigh that started down in her toes. "That's when it all comes out in the open, when they fall for a baby. I can remember my pal Jenny copping for a baby with a married man and it was awful. Her dad waited outside the man's workplace and gave him a damned good-hiding. Then the bloke's wife went round to Jenny's house and started screaming and shouting. You could hear her all over Radford."

"Did the married bloke leave his wife then?" Alf finished the remainder of his tea and held out his cup for more.

"No," Maisie poured more tea, "he packed Jenny in and her mam and dad had to bring the baby up."

"There you are, that's what I've just told you. The married blokes nearly always stick to their wives." Alf sniffed loudly. "Is my dinner about ready? If you don't hurry and give me my fish you'll have all the cats in Sodom hanging around."

Maisie prepared Alf's dinner and decided to say nothing more about Jack's affair. Well, not to any earthly being, she thought solemnly, but I could have a word with God, see if he can do 'owt to help.

Maisie had not prayed since the day her grandsons had died. Now seems like a good time to give him another chance, she thought, everybody ought to get another chance. She chopped parsley for the sauce and felt a bit happier.

★ ★ ★ ★ ★ ★ ★ ★ ★ ★ ★ ★

CHAPTER NINETEEN

Autumn days gathered in the sunny hours more quickly and early mornings embraced swirling carousels of mist.

In Radford nothing had changed much; jobs and money were still short but people held on and managed the best they could; helped each other and dreamed of better days.

The Evening Post held headlines and news items which gave more than a hint that something terrible was happening in Europe. The rest of the world seemed to be in a mess. Jack and his fellow workers discussed the world situation everyday in the canteen.

Names like Franco, Mussolini, Chiang Kai-shek and Hitler were becoming as well-known to the ordinary working men as the names of favourite film-stars were to their wives.

In Germany, young men dressed up in uniforms and called themselves the Hitler Youth. Factories pinned slogans on the walls about rearmament. "Guns before Butter" they urged. A campaign called the "Battle for Work" was thought up and workers flocked to the factories eager for any kind of work even if it was for making weapons of war. Trade unions and all political parties were closed down and Jewish people were persecuted; their shops were burned and smashed and they were attacked in the streets.

Jack always read every word about the problems abroad and one evening, as he was passing Mrs. Cohen's house on his way to a clandestine meeting with Iris, Jack heard something that swamped his body with a feeling of foreboding.

"Lovely evening, Mrs. Cohen. Looks like somebody's set the sky on fire doesn't it! Been a nice day though....what I've seen of it mind you. Stuck inside the factory most of it." He stopped to have a few words with the lonely old lady.

Mrs. Cohen, seated at her doorway, nodded and smiled at him.

"You mustn't grumble too much, Mr. Denbey. At least you have a job to go to and you're more-or-less free to lead your own life."

Jack sensed something was wrong and did not move away.

"Everything all right is it, Mrs. Cohen? Your Sammy keeping well is he then?" Jack tried to sound nonchalant.

Mrs. Cohen started the peculiar rocking from side-to-side and her eyes held the look of an animal which was being hustled towards a slaughter-house.

"He's been sent to a camp of some sort. Some sort of camp they said. I've had a letter from my cousin's boy and he said Sammy's gone to live in a camp. What do you think he's gone there for, Mr. Denbey? Last letter I got he never mentioned anything about no camp to me."

Rock, rock, rock she went, reminding Jack of a mother nursing an imaginary baby. Maybe it was Sammy she was nursing?

Jack knew he had to make up a white lie but could not think of one. He smiled, reassuring her, and at last answered, "They're doing a lot of re-organising in Germany at the moment, love. I was only reading about it the other day. I wouldn't be at all surprised if your Sammy doesn't get fed up and come back here to live. He could soon start another tailoring business up, couldn't he!" He put his hand on hers and patted it. "He could start up again anywhere, anytime. You needn't worry about much if you've got a bit of capital behind you. Your Sammy's not short of a bob-or-two, is he now."

"Yes, yes," Mrs. Cohen still looked afraid, "he could easily start another business here. He did well down Hyson Green."

"That's my ambition you know," Jack continued, "have my own little business somewhere. Where I could be my own boss....use my imagination. I hate being cooped up in a factory all day. It's like being caged up in one of them London zoos. I'm like a performing chimpanzee I am, duck."

"Perhaps you could work for my Sammy if he comes back to Radford."

"Now there's a good idea if ever I heard one. I could be his salesman. Vera says I've got the gift-of-the-gab."

They both laughed, Jack's polite and Mrs. Cohen's forced.

"Vera getting along all right, is she? No more problems?"

"Coming on a treat, thank you. It was just her nerves you know. Oh, I must get going now, Mrs. Cohen, got to meet a couple of pals of mine. Don't you worry about your Sammy, me duck. He'll probably come rolling down Denman Street in a taxi any day now. Flower in his button-hole, same as always."

Jack walked towards Denman Street thinking what a liar he had become. What was that piece of Robbie Burns he had once read! He tried to remember the lines. "I've got it," he concentrated and the words assembled themselves.

'Oh what a tangled web we weave
When first we set out to deceive'

I'm in a proper tangle and that's for sure, he thought unhappily. Lies to Vera everytime I want to get out to see Iris.

Then there were all those lies to Iris. Hinting about a possible future together and exaggerating about his life with Vera, and the unhappiness of their marriage, so that Iris would let him fondle and kiss her breasts.

Now I know what Jekyll and Hyde felt like, he mused. It's as though I'm living two lives at once and neither of them are what I really want. There's more to be had from life, I know there is, and I was meant to have it else I wouldn't feel so dissatisfied. All this play-acting's beginning to make me feel shabby and rotten. Relationships with women give you a sensation of emptiness somehow. He walked with his head down and did not notice his surroundings.

You have to work so hard at a relationship with a woman. It's just like they're draining me, between them. It's playing hell with my emotions. He found himself thinking about his mother, but his mind would not continue the blurred outline. Now he thought about Sammy Cohen then put a smile on his lips as Iris stepped out of a tobacconist's doorway and waved her hand.

★ ★ ★ ★ ★ ★

"I don't want to go down the allotments tonight," Iris patted at her hair which did not need patting and looked down the road; she would not look at him.

Jack still smiled at her but inside he felt dull and tensed up. He could sense he was in for another evening spoilt by one of Iris' peculiar moods. He sighed and waited for the old familiar dialogue that usually began with Iris saying she felt guilty and ending with Iris saying she was being used, and there then followed a tear-or-two for good measure.

Oh no....not tonight Iris, he thought. Not when men are being herded into terrible camps; not when I've just spent a beautiful sunny day staring at cigarettes taunting me with their endless dance.

Tonight I want warmth and gentleness. All the softness that women are supposed to be capable of giving. Tonight I want to talk about things that matter....things that matter to you inside. Tonight I want....oh, I don't know what the hell I want.

He lit a cigarette and flicked the spent match into the air.

"We can go for a drink then, if you like," he volunteered an alternative.

"Not bothered." A sulk cloud gathered over her left eye.

"Oh, we may as well, love. But we'll have to drink mild 'cause I'm a bit short again."

"Not bothered."

"Not bothered I'm short again?" he tried to make her smile. "We could walk up to the Borlace Warren and sit in the back room. Watch them play darts?"

"If you like....I'm not bothered."

That did it! The rappòrt between them vanished as quickly as a storm washes away a beautiful summer day; the affair floundered in the deluge of indifference. The magic and mystery had gone.

Jack felt as though a steam-roller had been on top of him and now, it had rolled away leaving him with a terrific feeling of light-headedness.

Who wanted black satin sheets — and red-gold hair! And leopardess' eyes were ten-a-penny. And sitting at the same machine as Iris all day long was too much like hard work. Ha-ha-ha. Double hard work if you ask me, he felt like making jokes even if they were about himself.

"What are you smiling at then?" Iris looked sulkier.

"I'm laughing at myself, love. Just laughing at myself. If you could take a patent out on me you'd make a fortune. I'm the biggest joke going."

"Oh well, if you're in that sort of mood."

"I'm always in the mood, you know that, Iris."

"And you can stop talking dirty."

"Yes, your dad wouldn't like it, would he!" Jack did not want to hurt her but he could not stop himself.

"Is it because I said I didn't want to go down the allotments, Jack?"

Jack could hear the coming-out-of-her-sulk overture but, like a man on the Wall-of-Death, he could not stop until he had pushed himself right up to the edge of disaster.

"I've been thinking, love. I'm getting a bit too old for a quick cuddle behind a green-house."

"You didn't think that last Thursday, you didn't. You made me ever so late home."

"I mean," Jack pretended to ignore her, "I've got a nice soft double-bed at home waiting for me, haven't I?" He knew he was being brutal but still he went on.

"Are you getting fed up with me then?"

"Nooooo," the tone of his voice said yes.

"You've only got to say," Iris played the wrong card, "'cause Roy Moore's asked me to go out with him. He's always asking me in fact. You've only got to say and we can pack in....I've been fancying Roy Moore for ages."

"You'd better go out with him then, hadn't you." The grand finàle at last.

They drank their glasses of mild but neither enjoyed the drink because thought had taken over from taste and reality had overpowered fantasy.

★ ★ ★ ★ ★ ★

Later that night Jack reached out for Vera as they lay side-by-side in the darkness. She responded to his caresses and Jack tried to wipe his mind free of all other thoughts as he entered her. But just before he went into his mind exploding climax, a kaleidoscope of images swirled through his head.

Iris' breasts and the secret, virgin place between her thighs; her feline, green eyes and the beautiful waterfall of red-gold hair. He imagined that it was Iris' voice which moaned softly from beneath him and again he saw the black satin sheets and her firm, white body.

Jack knew that Vera was pretending to enjoy his lovemaking and instead of putting him off, parodoxically, it aroused him more because he knew she cared enough to try to please him.

It was all blackness now and as he reached his climax, Jack felt as though life itself was gushing out of him. He covered his head with the sheet that smelled of starch and fresh air and thought sadly, that if he were a character in a book, none of the readers would like him very much. But I'm not all that bad, he argued with his conscience, I'm just an ordinary bloke who's been trapped by life around him. His mind would not switch off. Perhaps Vera would talk to him for a while!

"Goodnight Vera, love. All right are you?"

A sleepy yes from Vera, a moving of legs getting comfortable.

Jack closed his eyes and sighed deeply. In eight hours time he would be back amongst the cigarettes and that sickly smell.

I'll bet embalming fluid smells like our factory, he mused. Yes, it's a death smell all right. That's what it feels like to work in a factory, he tried to feel tired, it's as though you're embalmed; sort of half-dead and half-alive. He turned on to his other side.

I wonder if I could get a job down Sneinton Market! His mind would not give in to Morpheus. I wonder how you set about getting fixed up with a stall!

He fell asleep smiling and thinking, 'I'm not going to ask you for a shilling....not even ninepence, missis. 'Ere you are, duck....give me sixpence the lot.'

★ ★ ★ ★ ★ ★ ★ ★ ★ ★ ★ ★

CHAPTER TWENTY

"Don't mind if I go out for a couple of hours tonight do you, Vera?" Jack pushed his chair from the table and patted his stomach. "That was a lovely dinner. I could live on stew and dumplings if it came to the push."

"I thought I'd do a stew seeing as it's getting a bit nippy in the evenings." Vera stacked dinner plates and rattled cutlery. "Where are you going tonight then....out with the lads for a drink again?"

Jack nodded, was glad that it was the truth and the realisation put a smile on his lips. A darts-match was being held at the White Swan and Jack was giving support to a couple of pals from the factory.

Everyone liked a good darts-match with its mountains of sandwiches — cheese-and-onion, polony, haselet and potted-beef. And there were hot sausage-rolls sometimes, if the home-team won and the landlord felt generous.

Jack watched as Vera walked into the scullery with the pile of dirty pots.

"How'd you like to come with me, love? We could take Alex with us and he could play outside and have lemonade and crisps. They've got a bit of a place for kiddies at the back of the pub. They used to have a seesaw....I'll bet it's still there. Yes, let's all go, it'll make a nice change for you, love."

Vera agreed and was soon giving Alex's mouth a quick wipe with a flannel. She fussed with her hair then took out her new hat.

"I'll get done-up a bit then....give the neighbours a treat." She placed the hat on her head and tilted it to one side. "A hat's not a hat until it's tilted. Like my bunch of cherries, Jack?" The bunch of large red artificial cherries dangled jauntily over her left ear.

Jack was going to say he liked the hat whether he did or not but as he turned to look at her he felt a thrill of genuine pride.

The loss of the two boys and her nervous illness had scythed away all excess weight — her figure had regained its feminine ins-and-outs. The loss of flesh from her face accentuated the bone structure and Jack stared at the attractive face smiling at him from underneath the frivolous hat.

"Put your pearl necklace and ear-rings on as well. And your grey jumper and red coat. I always liked you in the red coat."

"Never thought I'd be able to get into that coat again." Vera sorted in the sideboard drawer for the artificial pearls.

"You look just like a film-star," Jack grinned at her, like he used to do, when they had been in love and silly. "We'll find you a seat near the dartboard and you can put all the blokes off their throws."

Flattery made her cheeks turn sunset pink and her eyes smiled for the first time in months.

An hour later Jack and Vera were walking down Edinburgh Street with an excited Alex skipping and jumping in front of them.

★ ★ ★ ★ ★ ★

Mrs. Cohen was seated at her usual place in the doorway.

"Hello, Mrs. Cohen," Jack smiled a greeting.

"Good evening, Mrs. Cohen," Vera did likewise and turned her head to one side so that Mrs. Cohen could have a good look at her new hat.

Mrs. Cohen did not return their smiles and for a few moments it seemed as though she was not going to speak to them either. She appeared to be in a trance and somehow, she looked unreal. Suddenly, she stood up and grabbed at Jack's arm.

"Come inside....come inside all of you." Her voice was so urgent Jack and Vera obeyed without thinking.

"I've been looking out for you, Mr. Denbey. Looking out for you I have." She gestured towards a deep-blue velvet sofa, Vera and Jack sat down, Vera lifted Alex onto her knee.

Mrs. Cohen closed the front door then also sat down in a matching velvet chair.

A few seconds and no words spoken; Jack coughed in a polite way and Vera fidgeted with Alex's socks.

"My Samuel has died."

The last few streaks of sunlight intruding into the room seemed to Jack like ice-cold straws; they sucked out all warmth from the room and the air felt chill and evil as though they were enveloped in a net of woven icicles.

Alex asked, 'when would they be going to the seesaw', but his childish voice, shrill and normal, still did not help.

"When did it er....happen, love?" What else could Jack say!

"Oh, I'm so sorry, Mrs. Cohen." Vera shared the death with her.

"I had a letter," Mrs. Cohen rocked, rocked, rocked; holding her son's lifeless body to her breast. "They sent a letter from Germany....from that camp where he'd gone to live. Pneumonia they said. He caught pneumonia." She leaned forward and stared into Jack's face.

"Do you think they'll send me his things? They ought to send me his belongings don't you think! His suit and shirts....and shoes."

Something to hold that had known his warmth; a shirt that had caressed his body; shoes that had covered his feet: the feet that had once been so reluctant to come out in to the world when she had thrust him from her womb head first into the light.

Mrs. Cohen looked at Alex and said, "I've got a nice bar of Fry's chocolate somewhere in my dresser drawer in the kitchen," she nodded towards the kitchen, "go and have a look and see if you can find it. Yes....it's all right," she smiled at him, "go and help yourself."

Alex wriggled free from Vera's arms and hurried off in search of the chocolate.

"What I wanted to say to you was this, Mr. Denbey," Mrs. Cohen relaxed a little. "You know what you said about working for my Sammy if he came back to Nottingham! What we talked about the other week! You saying as you'd like to have your own business, be your own boss! Well, I've got something for you and I don't want any arguing from you because I've made my mind up." She stood up, took her handbag from the top of the sideboard and handed Jack a large brown envelope. "I want you to take this gift from me. It's not a loan, but a gift because I'd like to help you along a bit."

Jack looked inside the envelope and gasped. Inside the envelope was a wad of five-pound notes.

"What's all this then?" Jack stared in disbelief at Mrs. Cohen then looked inside the envelope once again.

"It's three hundred pounds to help you to get started in your own business," Mrs. Cohen nodded and smiled at Vera. "You both deserve some help after what you've gone through. Such lovely boys....oh such lovely little boys," tears shimmered in her seen-it-all eyes, "such beautiful little boys," she was including her own son in the lament.

"But I can't take your money, duck!" Jack felt both anxious and elated. "I can't just take your money," he repeated, because his brain felt as though it had ceased to function properly, "I can't just take....!"

"No such word as can't, my father used to say. Please take it and make me very happy. My husband left me quite comfortable....I've more than enough to last me the few years I've got left. And I shall want you to let me know all about the business. Come and tell me about the profits and everything. If you want me to die a happy woman you'll have to make lots of profit. Now then, what do you say to a nice drink of sherry? Or perhaps you'd like a drop of mother's ruin, Mrs. Denbey?"

"Please call us Jack and Vera, Mrs. Cohen. Please....will you?" Jack looked embarrassed.

"Right you are then, Jack and Vera. Now, what are you going to drink?"

"Bottle of beer if you've got one please." Jack put the envelope on his knee and sat with his hands over it as though afraid it would disappear.

"Haven't got any beer, Jack. But you could fetch a jugfull from the White Swan if you like."

Jack walked to the pub swinging the white enamel jug from side-to-side. He felt as though a dentist had given him an extra large dose of gas. Laughing-gas in fact, he thought, because I feel like roaring with laughter. Three-hundred pounds....right out of thin air....and not even loaned but a gift from a lonely old lady who needed to buy a family of some sort. An old lady he and Vera had had time for — smiled at and asked after her son.

What was that bloke's name, he screwed up his forehead and tried to remember another poem. Him who said that, 'no man was an island. If the bell tolls it tolls for me'.

That bloke was right as well, he thought philosophically, we all need each other in life. And wasn't it funny how things seemed to work out right. It's like we're all standing in line waiting for God to give out nice times and bad times — and here I am right at the front of the good times queue.

He pushed open the door of the snug and ordered two pints of best bitter and four packets of crisps.

"John Donne," he said softly to himself, "John Donne."

"Yer what?" asked the landlord.

"I was just thinking," answered Jack, "it tolls for thee, for all of us."

"Huh, another one boozed up before he starts," whispered the landlord to his grinning barmaid, as Jack closed the snug door behind him and whistled "We're in the Money" as loud as his teeth would allow.

Jack, Vera and Mrs. Cohen, sipping their drinks and munching on crisps; no-one mentioned the darts-match, instead they talked about businesses, shops on the main road that had kept going and made good profits; they discussed the future venture like directors at a board-room meeting.

Jack confided to them that for a long time he had been nurturing the idea of having his own stall on Sneinton Market.

"I've been asking around in fact, thought I might be able to buy some stock with my next bonus from the factory. But it's quite difficult to get a stall down there apparently....mostly passed on from family-to-family. But with money behind me, well, there's a good chance I might be able to pull a few strings as they say. I could get a second hand lorry as well. Oh, I didn't say what sort of stall did I! Well, I had been thinking about a pot-stall. Somebody I work with used to do it and told me how to go about it. I know where they go to get the pots. There's a factory just outside Hucknall and then there's plenty of factories up in the Potteries....Stoke-on-Trent up that way. With a lorry of my own to fetch the things in it would be easy. There's a fortune to be made if you're prepared to work hard. I could work the markets all round the country once I got going. Sandiacre....Ilkeston....Birmingham even."

Mrs. Cohen nodded and rocked, nodded and rocked. Vera sipped gin-and-orange and her cheeks glowed with excitement in competition with the red of the cherries of her hat.

"I can't believe it's happening," she looked across at Mrs. Cohen, "I'm a bit frightened as well I can tell you. I'm a bit frightened of Jack giving up his job at the factory."

"No need to be, no need at all. I can tell your Jack's got drive. When my husband first started his tailoring business we had practically nothing. Parents helped of course, gave a little money to start us off, but the bank had to give us a loan, we had to borrow money. But you have nothing to worry about at all, Vera. Nice bit of capital behind you. I'll bet in a few years time you'll have enough to buy your own shop. A good class pot shop on Alfreton Road or Hyson Green. That's where all the money is....on the main roads."

"It'll not be for the want of trying if I don't make it pay, Mrs. Cohen. You've given me my big chance, the thing I've dreamt about for years and I'm not going to let go now. Would you mind if I smoked a cigarette, Mrs. Cohen. Smoke won't bother you will it!"

"Please do, Jack....my Sammy used to like a cigarette in the evenings. Liked the odd cigar as well he did. I can see him now puffing away on the things....I can...." her lips trembled.

"Blooming coffin-nails they are, Mrs. Cohen," Vera tried to help her, "and dangerous. Jack burnt a hole in the sofa the other week with one."

Jack tried not to think too much about Samuel Cohen. The room had lost its chill and a feeling of well-being had descended upon it instead. I'll never forget what happened to Sammy, he thought, but I don't want to think about it tonight. Tonight I want to savour all the good feelings I've got. This night is for living. There's plenty of time to be sad in the years ahead of me. Tonight, I'm at the front of God's good-times queue.

He lit the cigarette, blew the smoke into the air and thought, tomorrow I'll buy a few cigars....after all, businessmen have to look the part....a businessman with three hundred pounds behind him.

★★★★★★★★★★★★

CHAPTER TWENTYONE

Jack decided that his luck had changed for the best because he was being rewarded for no longer meeting Iris after work. He saw her at work of course, but now she was crazy about Roy Moore, a good looking trainee-fireman with a shy smile and gentle manner, who had all the girls desperate for a chance to go out with him. Iris had ensnared Roy with the same wiles that had caught Jack probably, Jack thought, and went hot as he thought about Iris' breasts and the beautiful young body. He envied Roy Moore his nights of ecstasy and passion with the beautiful Iris.

Iris had confided in the other girls, and Jack, that there would be an engagement ring on her finger by Christmas. That's what they need to keep them happy, Jack smiled to himself, engagement rings and wedding rings and pretty clothes — and a young, virile man the other girls longed for.

Jack still fantasised about Iris and realised it was because she had escaped; she would always be his dream woman; forever young, beautiful and unattainable. That was something Roy Moore would never have, he would see her grow old.

Roy Moore walked past the machine and smiled at Iris. Lucky young bogger, thought Jack, he won't know what's hit him once she's got him up the aisle. She was definitely a very passionate girl. A little bit inhibited, but hot blooded all the same.

The cigarette machines started out on their grinding journey for the day and Jack looked all round the room and smiled to himself. In a few minutes he would give in his notice to the foreman. It was all written carefully out and snuggling in an envelope inside his overall pocket.

Jack wanted to hang on to the letter as long as he could; look forward with delight to the look of astonishment that would appear on the foreman's face when he heard Jack say, here's my notice, see as it gets to the front office will you.

Jack had planned to say it loud so that he could also enjoy the expressions on the faces of the girls sitting half asleep at the machine.

He was not disappointed, all mouths opened wide like members of a choir just about to burst into song.

"Got a better job to go to, have you, Jack?" Bette was the first to recover.

"Not going off to fight the fascists, are you, Jack?" the foreman was sarcastic and looked jealous as well as surprised.

"We'll all miss you, Jack," Iris looked tearful but no tears came, she looked up the room for Roy Moore.

"Going into business on my own," Jack tried to sound nonchalant but his face was alive with excitement and secrets. "Actually, it all came about with something you said, Iris. Something you happened to mention about the stalls down Sneinton Market. Money to be earnt you said, if you remember. Well, I thought I may as well have a go. There's not much point sitting here till I drop dead....or waiting for the foreman to drop dead so's I can have his job," he looked meaningfully at the foreman. "So, I've got myself fixed up with a stall down the Market....and bought myself a lorry. Second hand job, but it'll do the trick. Get me to the Potteries and back."

The foreman held the letter in his hand and seemed unable to move. Jack knew that everything that was being said would be repeated and exaggerated in the front office; give those office wallahs something to think about, he thought happily. Little Gods in their pin-striped suits; silly sods poncing about with their stiff collars and stiff lips: zombies who changed into their flannels and sports-coats every Saturday morning because it was the done thing; copied the big bosses. Thought it made them look different but they still all looked the same. TRAPPED!! Poor boggers, Jack felt sorry for them now that he was escaping, the poor, poor boggers. He felt sorry for everybody in the factory; in fact, he thought he loved them all, he felt so sorry.

Jack held his head down because he was sure that everybody would know what he was feeling if they could see his face. And he felt so elated, so happy, it seemed terrible that everyone else should have such awful, miserable, drab lives, and he did not want to upset them further by letting them see his joy.

★ ★ ★ ★ ★ ★

Jack had given the man who had sold him the lorry a few shillings extra and in return the man had taught Jack to drive. Jack had soon got the gears and clutch sorted out and straight away he loved the feeling of power the driving gave him, sitting at the wheel in control of all that weight and throbbing engine.

It had taken nearly seven weeks for Jack to get a stall for himself and in the meantime he had hung around the Market every Saturday morning, got the feel of the atmosphere, listened to the patter of the stall-holders and chatted to the hawkers who stood around the periphery of the Market with their barrows.

There were already two established pot-stalls so Jack concentrated on them and listened and learned.

Working on one of the stalls was Fran, a dark-haired beautiful woman with eyes like a doe's, all soft and brown. She also had a quick witted tongue with patter that could sell a twentyfour-piece tea-set to a hermit.

"Come on, duck....six cups for twopence. Get plenty in for tonight to throw at your old man when he comes in drunk."

"And how about these lovely alsations! Beautiful aren't they, missis! If you can't afford to keep a dog as well as your 'usband, buy one of these instead.

I'm only asking two shillings, duck....it'd look lovely on top of the piano. And it won't wake the neighbours. Not if you don't chuck it at your 'usband when he's lost all his money on the horses it won't."

Fran also had a remarkable way of holding lots of pots in the crook of her arm then she would 'Pitch' as it was called, auction off tea-sets and dinner-services — starting with a ridiculously high price then coming down-and-down, getting the customers excited and clamouring to have such a wonderful bargain.

Jack practised holding the pots like Fran when he got home, but no matter how hard he tried he still could not manage anything like the number Fran could. She must have been trained by a magician, he thought one evening, after dropping one of Vera's best dinner plates with a crash.

★★★★★★

Jack's first Market-Day arrived and at a quarter-past seven on a misty, cold Monday morning three weeks before Christmas, Jack eased the gears into first and pointed the lorry in the direction of Hucknall.

One of the hawkers had told Jack about the pot factory just outside Hucknall so he had decided to go there first and leave the Stoke-on-Trent factories until later in the week when he had more time, then he could have a leisurely look round and search for bargains.

He arrived at the factory-gate well before eight o'clock and parked his lorry behind a variety of lorries and vans. Other stall-holders were helpful, told him where to go, who to see, what to look out for and things to avoid and at twenty to nine, Jack was heading for Sneinton Market laden with pots and ornaments.

The toll-man in charge of the Market had warned Jack that if he was not on his stall by ten o'clock the place would be given to someone else — one of the casuals who waited with laden barrows and five shillings, for the toll-man, just in case someone did not turn up.

At ten minutes past nine Jack parked his lorry at the side of the 'Mission Ragged Town School' which adjoined the swimming-baths and wash-houses; carefully he began to unload his pots and ornaments onto the stall.

Six tea-sets with ladies in crinolines painted all over them; one dozen alsations barking silently from half-open mouths; one dozen boys with patches on their knees, heads leaning backwards putting bunches of cherries into their mouths. Half-a-dozen art-deco ladies made from translucent glass, with long flowing hair and see-through green dresses, and holding dog-leads which had two green red-setters straining on the ends of them; one dozen chamber-pots with pretty cottages, complete with roses round the door, painted in the bottom; one dozen plain white ones.

Jack set the crockery out on the upturned wooden boxes and cardboard cases, arranged then re-arranged just like he had seen the other stall-holders do and kept a look-out for the customers.

The air was soon filled with the cries of the other stall-holders. "'Ere you are, duck....a nice rabbit. Shot it myself with a bow-and-arrow at three o'clock this morning. Only two bob and you can wear its feet as a lucky charm."

"Come on now ladies, real silk knickers, only one-and-six. Cost you five shillings on Long Row. Something to suit everybody here. Elastic in the legs for the married ladies....no elastic in the leg for the girls who are doing a bit of courting....and barbed-wire for the spinsters."

A young couple approached Jack's stall and looked interested in one of the crinoline lady tea-sets.

"Five shillings for a whole tea-set, love. Matching cream-jug and sugar-bowl so's you can be posh when your mother-in-law comes to tea. I've only got a few left and I don't think there'll be anymore like it 'cause they told me at the factory that the palace had snapped the others up for one of their Garden-parties. You'll have to crook your little finger like they do at the palace if you drink out of these cups, duck."

The young man was reaching inside his pocket, counting out the five shillings. Jack wrapped the tea-set in newspaper and tried to stop his fingers from trembling. The worst part was over — his very first sale — and it had been quite easy. He felt more confident. After writing down the sale in a note-book Jack smiled at a harassed looking woman who had two small children holding on grimly to her coat.

"'Ow much are yer pittle-pots, duck? It's getting too cold to walk across the yard in this weather. And the lav'll be freezing up soon 'an all." She picked up one of the decorated chamber-pots and scrutinised it. "How much are these....the ones with the cottages....? I 'ad one like this but I knocked it and the 'andle come off in me 'and. I'd 'ad it years an' all. It was a wedding present from me grandma."

"That one's a shilling, love," Jack tapped it with his pencil, "real china these are, duck. All the posh people use these sort."

"I'm not bothered about real china," the woman frowned and looked round the stall, "I don't want to pay as much as that. Haven't you got any pot ones? A good strong pot one'll do me."

Jack reached into a cardboard box and took out a plain white chamber-pot.

"Ninepence this one then." He bent down again. "Or, you can have this one for sixpence. It's got a small crack in it so I'll knock you threepence off."

"I don't want one with a crack in, me duck. Not the way my 'usband drinks Shippo's on a Sat'day night! You wouldn't dare have a crack in a dam now would yer! I'll have the ninepenny one, and 'ave you got a couple of cheap dinner-plates? Rejects'll do me. I don't mind if there's a few flowers missing off the edges. You can't eat the flowers, can yer, duck!"

Jack wrapped her purchases in newspaper and once again wrote the prices into his note-book.

It began to drizzle with rain but Jack did not seem to notice. Enthusiasm kept him warm; excitement and the newness of everything pumped the adrenalin around and around his body.

Things were going well for Jack and the rest of the stall-holders. Customers were stocking up for Christmas — replacing crockery and purchasing gifts they thronged all over the Market-place and Jack was disappointed when the hands of the clock above the school-house swizzled round to twelve-o'clock.

"Start packing a few things away now, Jack," a second-hand clothes dealer on the next stall to Jack gave advice. "Think you'll make it pay? You want to get yourself a barrow for the rest of the time you're not standing market. That's what a lot of the others do. Me and the missis take a barrow into the city centre and sell flowers and fruit mid-week and on a Saturday afternoon. Keep a good look out for the coppers though. They hound you a bit but if you get a good look-out you can scarper' fore they catch you. That's where you can make a bit of money, on the barrows. My family have been hawkers for years. I used to be a look-out for our dad, stood on Long-Row we did, good pitch."

Jack stored away inside his mind the idea of buying a barrow and decided to find out more.

"We're nipping across to Minnie's càfe for a cup of tea when we've finished, Jack. Minnie does a full meal and a good cup of tea....all for a shilling."

Market-day was packed swiftly away by the stallholders; green tarpaulin slithered down from the metal frames surrounding the stalls; coins were transferred from trouser pockets and pinafore pockets to boxes and handbags; pots were packed and vegetables stacked; customers disappeared quickly as holidaymakers at the seaside surprised by a sudden storm.

Jack put the remainder of his pots and ornaments into their boxes and stacked them back on to his lorry then he walked across to Minnie's cafe and ordered the full-course meal. Monday was Vera's wash-day and Jack hated the disorder it brought to the house so decided to keep away as long as he could.

After eating his meal Jack parked the lorry on the piece of waste-land known as 'Brassey' at the back of Independent Street and walked down to Mrs. Cohen's house to tell her how the business was going on.

"You wouldn't believe the change in her," he told Vera later that afternoon, "she looks ten years younger. She listens to every single word I'm saying and is as eager as though it was her stall I was working."

"It's given her an interest in life," Vera answered him, "you've taken the place of her Sammy. But be careful....don't let her get too much of a hold on you. I know she gave you the money but that doesn't mean she owns you."

Vera looked anxious but Jack smiled.

No need to worry about that, he thought, the woman's not born yet who could own me.

Tuesday, Jack spent a lot of time looking round the factories in the Potteries and was delighted to find lots of bargains. Tea-sets which had decorations missing or uneven patterns and rough edges, were being sold for three-shillings and half-a-crown. Ornaments, both china and pot, were reduced because of slight defects — Jack loaded the bargains onto his lorry.

On Wednesday, he set out early for the Sandiacre Market and got a good pitch just inside the entrance. His takings amounted to over five pounds more than he had collected at Sneinton on the Monday.

★★★★★★

Thursday tea-time, Jack visited Bert and Annie his neighbours and put forward an idea to Bert.

"How'd you like to help me on the markets, Bert? You could earn a few bob, and you'll not get rich on your dole money."

Bert did not reply but his delighted expression answered 'yes'.

"I need somebody to be my look-out as well," Jack continued, "because I've bought myself a barrow."

Bert and Annie sitting side-by-side on the sofa were transfixed by the news.

"If you want to work for me, you'll have to get up early and go down the market to snap up the bargains. And I'll have to teach you to drive the lorry as well."

"I can drive...I can drive," Bert enthused, "I used to drive a lorry in France.... in the war."

"Right then, if you're interested you can start work next Monday morning, I should have got everything sorted out by then. You can stand Sneinton Market with me and then we'll take the barrow into the city centre and see how we go. You'll need to wrap up warm....it's a bit nippy standing the market this weather."

"I can't believe I'm hearing proper. I've always wanted a job where I'm driving summat. Didn't I say to you, Annie, as I'd like a job driving summat!"

Annie's bulging-out-of-blouse breasts heaved up and down with excitement.

"Yes, you did love, and you should be all right driving a barrow," she winked at Jack then looked serious. "It's very good of you to think of Bert. We'd just been saying that we weren't looking forward to Christmas 'cause we haven't got two halfpennies to rub together. The money goes nowhere nowdays. It was very good of you to think of him."

"Oh, don't worry, I'm not daft you know. Your Bert's got a lively personality and that's what I want on the market. Somebody who can push the pots and nic-nacs, I thought of Bert straight away. And also, I'm like an elephant! I don't forget a kindness. You and Bert were as good-as-gold to Vera when she first came out of the 'Big-House'. I know who the neighbours are who looked at the pavement when they saw her coming down the street. And those who smile at her in a supercillious way as though she's batty."

"That's a good word, Jack," Annie stood up, took the blackened-with-soot kettle off the hob and set it down on top of the roaring fire. "I don't know what it means, but it sounds good." She laughed and added, "And I'll bet it's made you thirsty using big words like that. Supercillious!"

They all laughed, the true laughter of good-naturedness, and waited for the kettle to boil.

★★★★★★

"I've asked Bert if he wants to help me and he's jumped at the idea." Jack told Vera the news and she was pleased. Jack put his arm around her.

"What do you say to a quick half at the Red Lion? We can wait till Alex's gone off to sleep. He'll be all right for an hour."

"All right then, Jack. Let's call for Bert and Annie as well."

At half-past ten that night Jack and Bert could be heard all over Independent Street as they sang in ale lubricated voices 'Keep Young and Beautiful if you Want to be Loved'.

"SHURRR-UUUP", shouted one or two voices from the safety of their bedrooms, in chorus with a few barking dogs.

The following Saturday Jack set his stall out once again on Sneinton-Market and this time he used more salesmanship, pushed the sales of his goods, and the more he did so the more his confidence grew. He stood on a box and in a loud voice told the customers about the wonderful bargains he had waiting for them for the price of a few coppers.

People drifting up the stall then drifting away again, reminding Jack of flotsam and jetsam tossed backwards and forwards by the tide; occasionally anchoring to the side of his stall, selecting pots and ornaments then ebbing away again into the sea of bodies and noise.

At one o'clock Jack stacked all the unsold goods onto his lorry then walked across to Minnie's cafe for a hot, wholesome, three-course meal. You need some 'snap' inside you working outside in this weather, he told himself, and if I get a pitch on Ilkeston-Market I shall need plenty of packing inside me.

★ ★ ★ ★ ★ ★

Ilkeston market-place was bustling with people when Jack arrived.

"I can just fit you in if you take that space over there," the toll-man pointed to an empty site.

Jack set out his stall once again and waited for the customers. Late afternoon squeezed daylight from the skies and a cold dampness made men turn up jacket collars and women pull woollen scarves tighter.

Flare-lamps were lit and hung at the ends of the stalls — as darkness triumphed over light the flickering, dancing flames reminded Jack of huge fire-flies.

"You'd better get yourself a couple of lamps, mate." A man selling secondhand boots and shoes on the next stall called out to Jack.

"Where can I get a couple, do you know?" Jack called back to him.

"Nip over to Nellie's hardware shop. Next to the chip-shop across the road there," he pointed to a row of shops, "I'll watch yer stall."

Jack hung the acetylene lamps on the ends of his stall, turned them up high. So much to learn, he thought, but I'll soon master it, just watch me. He looked at the throng of people shuffling up-and-down the aisles; picking up and putting down; bargaining and giving in: a Saturday ritual to be lingered over and enjoyed.

This is what you call working for a living, now I feel as though I'm living as well as working. Jack lit a cigarette and sat down on one of the wooden packing-cases. Breathe the fresh-air instead of the nauseating smell of tobacco — meet different people instead of being imprisoned with the same giggling bunch of girls all day long. Enjoy the comradeship of other stallholders instead of enduring the nastiness and pettiness of a bird-brain foreman.

Jack watched with pleasure as cups, saucers, plates, chamber-pots and ornaments left empty spaces on his stall. He thought he had never experienced anything so thrilling in his life as fingering the money mounting up inside his trousers' pockets.

"I'm ready for a pint aren't you, mate!" His neighbour blew on clenched fists and stamped his feet.

"Drop of rum or whisky'd be more like it," Jack called back.

★ ★ ★ ★ ★ ★

At half-past eight the cries of the stallholders grew louder as they tried to sell off as much as they could before the market closed at nine o'clock.

"Hot taters....only a few left....hot taters."

"'Ere y'are love....a nice rabbit for tomorrow's dinner."

"Who wants some nice crisp celery! Two for the price of one. Crisp celery....break yer false teeth on it."

"Who'll buy this beautiful fur coat! Thirty bob! Come on love....you'll look like two dogs having a fight when yer walk down the street in this."

"Come on ladies....get yourselves done-up tonight. Lovely blouses just like Ginger Rogers wears. Your old man'll tap-dance you straight upstairs to bed if you wear one of these. Half-a-crown to dress like a film-star....come on ladies....two bob then....you'll bleddy ruin me."

"Who wants a nice meat-pie for their supper! Come on girls....they don't call me Sweeney Todd for now't. Few chips and peas with it and your 'usband'll think he's dining out at the Ritz."

"Tripe....pig's trotters....brawn....haselet! 'Ere y'are, missis....come on now....who wants some collared-'ead with hairs on! Makes yer hair curl, missis!"

Cries died away, flare-lamps were extinguished one-by-one and instead, the night was brightened by the cheerful glow from public-houses, beer-offs and street gas-lamps.

Jack sat at the wheel of his lorry and paused before turning the ignition-key.

The air had turned much colder and crispness replaced the dampness. A moon, round and yellow turned the corner of a cloud and Jack, motionless inside the lorry murmured softly to himself — as a Thespian learns lines in the quietness of a bedroom.

'There was a time when meadow, grove and stream,
The earth, and every common sight,
To me did seem
Apparelled in celestial light'.

"Old Wordsworth knew," Jack turned the ignition-key and pulled out the starter-button, the lorry rumbled with life, "he must have felt just the same way as I'm feeling right this minute."

The lorry rattled its way along roads flanked by trees and half-hidden farmland and soon, Jack saw the fire-fly lights of Nottingham twinkling and beckoning to him.

He pressed his foot on the accelerator and sped towards Vera; a pint of ale; a hot supper: and a soft, soft bed.

★ ★ ★ ★ ★ ★ ★ ★ ★ ★ ★ ★

CHAPTER TWENTYTWO

"Here you are, Jack....drink your tea before it gets cold." Vera drew back the bedroom curtains and continued, "You didn't half sleep soundly last night, I could hardly hear you breathing at all, and you went out like a light."

"I should think so as well," Jack struggled to an upright position and reached for his teacup, "I didn't stop from half-past six in the morning till gone nine last night. But as I told you, it was worth it. I shifted nearly all the stuff. I'm going to nip round to Mrs. Cohen's while you're cooking the dinner....tell her how I went on yesterday."

Vera sat on the edge of the bed and looked down at the eiderdown.

"Jack, while you're in a good mood, I want to tell you something. You know when we had that row....that time when I told you I was having another baby! Well, I'd like you to know that I didn't mean all the awful things I said to you. I don't hate you touching me. It was just that I felt so desperate, catching again so soon after having Alex."

"I know, you don't have to draw me a map, love. I said some horrible things to you as well. And I didn't mean them either."

"I felt worn out, Jack. Absolutely worn out. Well, what I'm trying to tell you is this. I wouldn't mind having another baby now. If you think your stall is going to be a success that is. I don't want you worrying about money all the time. Do you think it will make money?"

"Oh, the stall will do well you needn't bother about that. And wait till I get cracking with the barrow as well. I'll have a little bet with you that this time next year we'll be able to afford a car to run about in. How would you like to nip over to Skeggy or Blackpool in a posh Austin Ten? Their eyes'll pop out their heads on Independent Street when they see us pulling up in an Austin Ten."

Vera smiled at him and answered, "You've got some big ideas haven't you! Our own car in a year's time!"

"You've said it, kid. I've got a feeling that 1939 is going to be our year."

Vera was only half listening to him.

"If I did catch for another baby, perhaps it would be a little girl. Oh Jack, I've always wanted a little girl."

"What's all this babies stuff then?" Jack took hold of her hand, "how about coming back to bed for half an hour?"

Vera laughed and with a girlish gesture pulled her hand away.

"I've got the breakfast to cook and Alex is prowling about. But we could have half an hour when Alex's gone to Sunday School."

"The Lord will provide," laughed Jack, "the Lord will provide." But he was not being blasphemous — just happy, carefree and confident that the Lord was at last on his side.

★ ★ ★ ★ ★ ★

"I knew you would do well....I could tell you were a born businessman." Mrs. Cohen sipped her sherry and smiled widely, showing the pink part of her dentures as well as her teeth. "You would have made a good partner for my Sammy," pain wrenched the smile from her face, "they still haven't sent me his belongings. I have heard nothing....not one word from that camp place."

"Oh dear, I am sorry, Mrs. Cohen," Jack tried to think of something to say that would take her mind off Sammy, "I'm going to take the barrow out tomorrow afternoon, when I've finished down Sneinton." She smiled again and forgot about her Sammy for a while.

"Don't think many people'll buy flowers on a Monday," Jack continued, "so I'm going to have a bash with some vegetables and fruit. A bloke who lives up our yard is going to be my look-out. And he's going to help on the stall as well. He's on the dole so I'm going to give him a few bob on the quiet at first, see how things go. If everything goes all right, I'll set him on as a regular, pay proper wages, but it's early days yet." Jack sipped at his beer. "Do you know, Mrs. Cohen....you've opened up a whole new life for me....a whole new world in fact," he beamed a smile at her, "you're my guardian angel. They say everybody's got one don't they! Well you're mine love, and may God bless you for all you've done to help me."

"Pooh, don't call me an angel. I'm not ready for cocking my toes up just yet. Fancy you making all that profit, Jack. Are you sure you added it up right?"

"Dead right, love. But don't forget it's nearly Christmas. Things'll go quiet after Christmas. I'm going to get some Christmassey things to sell on the barrow next week. Some mistletoe, handkerchiefs in boxes, all that sort of thing. The stuff they snap up at Christmas."

"Oh....you sound just like my Samuel," she smiled delightedly and rocked from side-to-side, "he loved talking business."

I'll be him if you want me to, thought Jack, I'll take his place if that will help you.

Jack lit a cigar and talked about making money — just like Samuel Cohen used to do. He refilled her sherry glass and thought how little it took to make the lonely old lady happy for a while.

★ ★ ★ ★ ★ ★

"I reckon it'll snow before the day's out," Bert breathed on his clenched fists then bashed then up-and-down on his thighs, "it wouldn't surprise me."

"Push those alsation-dogs, Bert." Jack rearranged a few ornaments. "And push the tea-sets with the lilies-of-the-valley on. And I want to try and get rid of the brown pudding-dishes. If we can shift that lot we'll be laughing. There's a few faults on the plates and saucers but there's a hundred-per-cent profit on each sale if we get what we're asking for them."

"Right, Jack." Bert moved an alsation-dog to the front of the stall and looked out at the crowd. "Alsation-dogs....here you are, missis....a special bargain seeing as it's nearly Christmas. Two bob, and I haven't just escaped from the loony-bin. I'm in a generous mood today I am, the missis has give me a promise for tonight." He banged on the side of a box. "I'll tell you what I'll do with you, ladies! If you buy one of these beautiful tea-sets, I'll let you have a dog for a tanner."

Jack gave him a peculiar look and frowned.

"No....I'll go one better, girls," Bert had their attention, "if you buy one of these beautiful tea-sets, they're just like the ones they use at the Kardomah.... I'll let you have one of these lovely dogs," he held a pot alsation-dog high above his head, "one of these lovely ornaments for," he banged on the box again, "for nothing."

The crowd surged nearer and women pushed one another.

"Here you are, ladies....two bargains for the price of one. Five-bob and they're both yours for the asking, but I've only got ten tea-sets so you'd better fight it out amongst yourselves."

Hands holding coins were thrust towards Bert — he took the money and nodded at Jack.

"Wrap them up, Jack, before I come to my senses," he looked into the crowd and shouted, "I think I need a lie down in a darkened room, missis."

"What....with a blonde!" a wit from the back of the crowd shouted back.

Ten tea-sets and ten alsation-dogs disappeared into the crowd and Jack grinned at Bert and said, "You catch on quick, Bert."

"Oh, I've watched how they operate. Frightened you did it, when you thought I was giving the dogs away for nothing?"

"Yes it did, you daft bogger. I didn't know what the hell you were doing. I thought you were going to let the tea-sets go for three-shillings, the proper price."

"Sprat to catch a mackerel," Bert handed the money to Jack, "what do you want shifting next?"

"Some of those lads eating cherries," Jack answered, "I'm sick of looking at them. They cost me one-and-three each, so if we can get half-a-crown for them I'll be happy....or two bob if we're pushed."

"Right then, half-a-crown it is."

"And push those brown rice-pudding dishes. I bought three dozen of them, let them go for fourpence, they only cost me twopence."

"Neb-u-chad-nez-zar
The king of the Jews
Bought his wife a pair of shoes
When the shoes began to wear
Neb-u-chad-nez-zar
Began to swear"

Children's voices spiralling over the wall of the 'Mission Ragged Town School' and cascading down over the Market.

"One potato, two potatoes, three potatoes, four
Five potatoes, six potatoes, seven potatoes, more."

Skip, skip, skip, went the tiny feet as they jumped over pieces of clothesline. Feet thrust into shoes that were too small; feet slithering about in shoes that were too large; feet that were itching with chilblains and burning with blisters.

"When the shoes began to wear
Neb-u-chad-nez-zar
Began to swear."

"It's their playtime," Bert nodded towards the school, "don't they make a row?"

"Like dogs let off the lead," Jack looked solemn, "did you see the state of some of them this morning? Some of their clothes were hanging in rags. Poor little boggers looked starved to death."

"No different to me, Jack, when I went to school," Bert stamped his feet up-and-down to keep warm, "my trousers arse was always hanging out. And I didn't have any shoes either, not in the summer. And them I did have, were secondhand. I've got a bloody great bunion to remind me as well. You'd have thought after a war things would have got better, but I can't see much difference, can you, Jack?"

"I'll make sure our Alex gets more from life than we did," Jack answered, "if I have to push a barrow from here to Timbuktu, I'll make sure of that." He reached into his trousers pocket and took out a shilling. "Here you are, Bert. Nip across to Nellie's cafe and get two mugs of tea and a couple of bacon sandwiches."

"On the mountain, stands a lady
Who she is, I do not know.
All she wants, is gold and silver
All she wants, is a nice young man.
So call in my Billy dear
Billy dear, Billy dear
So call in my Billy dear
While I go out to play."

The children's voices, sounding vital and happy, made a lump in Jack's throat so large that he had to cough out loud before it choked him.

All she wants is gold and silver, he repeated the words in his mind. All they want is a hot meal and some warm clothes, he thought sadly, not much to ask from life, is it! He reached for a statue and held it in the air.

"Come on now, duck....you'll not get a better bargain anywhere. These statues are all the go in America and on the pictures. They have them in all the Busby Berkeley musicals. And Fred Astaire and Ginger Rogers.... Marlene Deitrich....and Greta Garbo, they've all got them in their houses. Here....give me two shillings for one and I'll let you have one of these lovely ashtrays absolutely free. Stop your old man flicking his ash on the best

Wilton, missis."

He held the Art-Deco ladies high in the air and waved them about.

"I daren't go any lower than one-and-ninepence, duck. Here you are then, one-and-ninepence and a free ashtray."

"When the shoes began to wear
Neb-u-chad-nez-zar
Began to swear."

I'll make sure I'll never want for money again....not if I have to push a barrow for the rest of my life, Jack thought. And I'm free....free to come-and-go as I like. Let Vera have the fancy furniture and all the things that keep you trapped. If it keeps her happy having nice things in the house that's what she can have. I'll settle for my freedom.

He wrapped two Art-Deco ladies in newspaper and sorted in the box for another pair.

Bert returned with the bacon sandwiches and mugs of tea.

"Are you making it pay, Jack? I've been a help to you, have I?" Bert munched on a piece of crispy bacon and warmed his hands on the hot mug.

"Not bad at all, Bert. I'll be able to let you have a few bob when we've been out with the barrow this afternoon. Providing we don't get nicked by the coppers. Keep your eyeballs on the swivel, Bert. We don't want nicking and have a fine to pay."

"I'll have eyes in the back of me arse, Jack, don't worry about that. If you can let me have a few bob, I'm going to take our Annie to the pictures tonight. They've got a George Formby on at the Lenos."

"Oh, that soft bogger....Vera goes to see all his pictures. What's this one called then, on at the Lenos?"

"Feather Your Nest I think Annie said it was called."

"Never mind about George Formby! It's us who are going to do that, mate." Jack chewed on the last of his sandwich, drank the remainder of his tea and called out to the crowd, "'Ere you are, girls....lovely earthenware dishes. Just the thing to cook your old man's pudding in. I'm not asking a shilling or ninepence....I'm giving them away for a tanner." He banged on the side of a box, "not even a tanner....here you are, girls, fourpence for a genuine earthenware pudding-dish."

"And you can join our Pudding-Club if you'll step this way, ladies," Bert joined in, "who wants a bun-in-the-oven! Step this way, girls."

Women laughed and held up their money. Jack sorted underneath the stall for the statues of 'lads eating cherries' just as the children flooded out of the school-gates opposite; a tidal wave of thin legs; thin arms; thin faces: thin clothes.

"Watch it, Jack," called the man on the greengrocery stall next door, "they pinch stuff that lot do."

"Right," Jack called back to him, "I'll keep my eye on the little boggers then." But he thought that it did not seem like a crime, not when you were poor and hungry. Not as bad as adultery or telling lies when you analysed it — you could stop yourself making love to another bloke's wife and nobody forced you to tell lies — but you couldn't help being hungry and poor.

"'Ave yer got any owd pots you don't want, mester?" A Sneinton child, with the haunted look of poverty and dull, weighing-you-up eyes stood at the side of Jack's stall.

"Clear off," said Bert gruffly.

"Go on....give us a plate." The child leapt up and agile as a monkey, caught hold of the metal framework surrounding the stall and began to swing himself up-and-down, thin legs jerking rhythmically from out of patched trousers that were two sizes too large.

Jack caught hold of him and lifted the wriggling body down. He pressed a threepenny-bit into the surprised child's hand and said quietly, "Go and get yourself a cup of tea and a bun. And don't get telling your pals either, because there's no more where that came from." He raised his voice louder and added, "Clear off, you young bogger or I'll kick your arse."

The scrap of rags disappeared into the crowd as Jack joined in with Bert and cried out, "This way ladies for the bargains....who wants a nice tea-set, like they use at the Kardomah. Here you are, girls....tea-sets covered in roses....look lovely in the best cabinet."

★★★★★★★★★★★★

CHAPTER TWENTYTHREE

"I thought your mam looked a bit weary last week," Jack looked up from the Evening Post, "how about having the party here on New-Year's-Eve, give her a break?"

"Oh, I don't think so, Jack. Mam's always had a party on New-Year at her house, no matter how poor we've been, she's always managed to arrange something. She's already invited Nellie Tealeaf and Bill Davenport. They look as though they're getting serious by the way! He bought Nell a lovely brooch for Christmas. It was silver because I saw the hall-mark stamped on it." Vera knitted to the end of a row.

Jack put his newspaper down and lit a cigarette. He spat a piece of loose tobacco in the direction of the fire-grate.

"I'm going to give up smoking as my resolution. I'll have the odd cigar now-and-then, but I'm going to give up fags. It's daft paying out good money and watch it go up in smoke. It was all right while I was getting them free from the factory, but I begrudge paying for them. Now then, about this party! We could invite Maisie and Alf and Nellie and Bill Davenport. And Bert and Annie could come round as well and I could fetch Mrs. Cohen. We can't leave Mrs. Cohen on her own on New-Year's-Eve. What do you think, love? I'll have a word with Maisie if you like. I'll bet she'd be glad of the break."

"I don't think she'd want to break from the usual routine."

"Well, we can always suggest it. We'll ask her and Alf to tea in the afternoon, light a fire in the front-room and they can have a nap in there before the others arrive. And we'll let Alex stay up till midnight seeing as he's a bit older."

"All right then, you have a word with mam and Alf and see what they say. It's ages since we had a party here. I could make a trifle and bake sausage-rolls and things. Can we afford some spirits?"

"Of course we can. I've still got a few quid left from Christmas. And there's some money left out of Mrs. Cohen's three hundred. I want to leave it in the bank though if I can, towards a deposit for the car. I've set my mind on a car. Did I tell you I made two hundred per cent profit on the celery and fruit?"

"Yes you did, but I still feel cautious, Jack. Are you sure things won't die down a lot now Christmas has gone?"

"Now what did I tell you about Fran, the 'Queen of the Pots' and Maude, the 'Queen of the Lino'! They've been working on the market for years and are still making a good living."

"Do you think I could have a new coat then? I don't mind waiting till the January sales."

"You can have a new coat with pleasure, my love. Have you seen one you like then?"

"Yes, in Marks & Spencers....a lovely dark brown with a big fur collar."

"There aren't any Markets anywhere tomorrow so I'll take you to try it on in the morning. I'm not taking the barrow out till the afternoon. Going to buy some more oranges and bananas off the Smedleys. If I have six crates of each they let me have them cheaper than the shops get them for."

"Shall we have an early night, Jack!" Vera smiled at him.

"I'm game if you are," Jack smiled back, "but let me nip round to The Oak for a jug of ale first. I could just fancy a drink of beer, couldn't you?"

Vera crossed her legs and showed off shapely calves. The promise of a new coat; the planning of a party; and the talk of having a fancy motor-car had created a good mood. She imagined herself walking down Independent Street in the dark brown coat and decided to buy a perky dark brown hat to go with it.

Jack switched on the bedside-lamp and walked over to the window — he took hold of the curtains.

"Don't draw the curtains," Vera spoke softly, "switch the bedside-light off and we'll just have the light from the gas-lamp."

Arms entwined they snuggled close and whispered kindly to each other, flattering pleasantries and courting words.

Jack's face had a nice smell of shaving-cream and Vera's body was embraced by Evening-in-Paris perfume.

Jack took time over his lovemaking and his passion became heightened by the genuine response from Vera's body.

As he entered her, without the off-putting indignities of contraception, for the first time in years Jack thought only of Vera. No imaginary visions of film-stars reclining on black satin sheets; no Iris with virgin body and tempting eyes and mouth; no writhing whore leading him into the delights of unspeakable depravity: this time he wanted to please Vera as well as satisfy himself and there was the added thrill of knowing that Vera wanted to become pregnant.

He tried to hold back, make the marvellous feeling last, the pain of self-control made him feel as though his head would burst right open. He tried to think of something else, hold back his climax so that when it did come it would be the best ever.

Vera was moaning beneath him — clutching at his back and pulling him further and further inside her. He gave up the fight and released thousands of would-be babies into the unknown and dowsed thousands of flashing lights from inside his head.

"She'll be born in the autumn," said Vera, before plunging into a deep sleep.

"Autumn....nineteen thirty nine....sounds like a good time....," Jack thought drowsily and murmured to himself, "a time to look forward to."

He tucked in the eiderdown to keep the draught from his back and also fell fast asleep.

★ ★ ★ ★ ★ ★

"Should auld acquaintance be forgot and never brought to mind
De dah...de dah...de dah...de dah
For the sake of auld-lang-syne."

Maisie, Alf, Nellie Tealeaf, Bill Davenport, Mrs. Cohen, Annie, Vera, Jack and Alex; holding hands, linking arms; shy in their friendship; happy in the knowledge of that friendship.

Jack turned up the wireless and the chimes of Big-Ben pushed away the old year and heralded the new.

A knock at the door, shouting and mock surprise as Bert stepped over the scullery step holding a lump of shiny black coal and a crust of freshly baked bread.

"Happy New-Year....Mrs. Cohen."

Rock, rock, rock from side-to-side, a nod of the head, a smile and a looking forward.

"Happy New-Year....Bert and Annie."

Arms around one another, a big smacking kiss and the hopes of a regular wage and better times.

"Happy New-Year....Bill and Nellie."

A holding of hands, a giggle and an embarrassed grin. Happiness late in life, but both feeling secure and wanted at last.

"Happy New-Year....Maisie and Alf."

Perhaps....said their eyes....perhaps!

"Happy New-Year....Jack and Vera."

A light kissing of cheek, secrets in their smiles. Maybe the crystal-ball held happiness at last!

"Happy New-Year....Alex."

It had to be. No more ragged, hungry children; away with dole queues; there would be equal opportunities for all and an end to wars.

"On the mountain stands a lady
Who she is I do not know
All she wants is gold and silver
All she wants is a nice young man
So call in my Alex dear, Alex dear, Alex dear...."

Nineteen-thirty nine will be the best year ever, thought Jack, as he lit a cigar and refilled the glasses.

★ ★ ★ ★ ★ ★ ★ ★ ★ ★ ★ ★